Companion

Samuel Rigel

Copyright © 2024 by Samuel Rigel

All rights reserved.

No portion of this book may be reproduced in any form without written permission from the publisher or author, except as permitted by U.S. copyright law.

Contents

1. Prologue — 1
2. Chapter 1 — 6
3. Chapter 2 — 12
4. Chapter 3 — 17
5. Chapter 4 — 22
6. Chapter 5 — 27
7. Chapter 6 — 32
8. Chapter 7 — 37
9. Chapter 8 — 43
10. Chapter 9 — 49
11. Chapter 10 — 55
12. Chapter 11 — 61
13. Chapter 12 — 67
14. Chapter 13 — 73
15. Chapter 14 — 79

16.	Chapter 15	84
17.	Chapter 16	89
18.	Chapter 17	95
19.	Chapter 18	101
20.	Chapter 19	106
21.	Chapter 20	112
22.	Chapter 21	117
23.	Chapter 22	123
24.	Chapter 23	129
25.	Chapter 24	135

Prologue

1 2 October, 1824 Bedfordshire, England

"Fiona!" Jeanette shouted, clutching her walking stick tightly as she ambled towards the entrance of their cottage. "Come back here, I say!"

"I will be late if I do, nana," her great granddaughter replied, her skirts almost half way up her calves as she clutched them—already on the run.

"You need to eat something, girl. And put your skirts down! How many times have I told you that it's unladylike to run like that?!"

"I'll find something to eat in the Duke's kitchens." She conveniently ignored the second sentence.

"You're a blight on the human race," she screamed.

"So are you! Now go back inside, I'll be just fine!"

Jeanette let out an exasperated sigh and turned around. She couldn't very well run behind the girl with a basket of breakfast at her age, could she?

Fiona ran like the very devil was behind her. It was her first day at work and she couldn't afford to make a bad impression.

She was to be a companion to the dowager duchess of Bedford. And Fiona was extremely nervous and excited. She previously served the Baroness Redgrave's mother—Lady Henrietta for five years—until the kind lady had passed six months back. Fiona hadn't had any source of income since then even though the Baron Redgrave had given her an excellent reference.

Until last week.

A letter had been delivered to her home by a sharply dressed footman. She'd jumped with joy when she'd seen the seal of the Duke.

A higher rank meant higher wages, after all.

Apart from being a womaniser, Baron Redgrave had been a stingy employer as well. But she'd stayed for Lady Henrietta.

The Duke had written that she would have a say in her wages. Which meant that Fiona could save enough to manage a decent enough feast for Nana Jeanette by Christmas.

She stopped running when she reached the woods. She couldn't afford to trip over something and hurt herself—not today.

Besides, she still had time. She began to sing to herself—a song she'd picked up from Lady Henrietta, truly happy for the first time in days.

"'Tis the last rose of summer,Left blooming alone;All her lovely companionsAre faded and gone;No flower of her kindred,No rosebud is nigh,To reflect back her blushes,Or give sigh for sigh.

I'll not leave thee, thou lone one!To pine on the stem;Since the lovely are sleeping,Go, sleep thou with them.Thus kindly I scatter,Thy leaves o'er the bed,Where thy mates of the gardenLie scentless and dead.

So soon may I follow,When friendships decay,And from Love's shining circleThe gems drop away.When true hearts lie withered,And fond ones are flown,Oh! who would inhabitThis bleak world alone?"

****

Nate was having a fine time riding his gelding this morning. The weather was lovely—the perfect day to escape even if it was for a few hours.

He lead his horse into the woods, it must be thirsty.

Once he spotted the stream, he dismounted and lead the horse towards the stream.

Nate looked about him, the air was crisp with a light chill. And the soil smelt fresh.

But even his beautiful surroundings didn't let him forget about his mother. He'd tried to reason with her but it was absolutely useless. She wasn't willing to listen to him—already having made up her mind.

They'd fought every single day this entire week. Ever since he'd informed of his decision to hire a companion for her. It had been a long time coming and he'd begun thinking about it sometime back but she'd refused to even discuss it, of course.

But the incident that took place last week sealed his decision.

She'd been trying to climb down the stairs in-spite of her arthritis. At the last few steps, the pain became too unbearable and she simply fell down.

The butler heard her shriek and immediately rushed there to find her lying on the floor, her face contorted in pain.

What pained him the most was that he hadn't been there for her. He'd been away in London when he heard the news.

Nate closed his eyes, a sudden ache bursting in his chest, making it difficult for him to breathe.

He didn't know why she was being so stubborn but he knew that this wouldn't have happened if she'd have had someone with her. He'd made up his mind and he wasn't going to change his decision.

An awful sound forced him to open his eyes. His hackles immediately went up. What was that?

He mounted his gelding and followed the sound, straining his ears. He navigated through the thick woods carefully, pushing a few branches out of his way.

And then he heard it properly.

"Where thy mates of the gardenLie scentless and dead..."

Some woman was butchering what he suspected was a very beautiful ballad by Thomas Moore.

He wanted to clutch his belly and laugh. He wanted to see who this woman was. And he wanted to thank her for improving his mood with her terrible singing.

Nate almost followed her further but then changed his mind at the last moment.

He would probably scare the poor woman with an unannounced appearance. Besides, he needed to reach his estate.

The companion he'd hired would arrive this morning and although Redgrave had only good things to say about her, Nate wasn't going to let a literal stranger near his mother. He'd have to take stock of the woman first.

So he changed his direction and took the short route to his estate.

When he reached home, he took off his greatcoat and asked his butler where his mother was.

"She said she didn't wish to see you, your grace," Winterbottom said stiffly. The butler had taken it as a personal affront that Nate didn't think he was good enough to care for his mother.

Nate sighed and nodded. "I will be in my study..."

"I shall send the woman there then, your grace," Winterbottom bowed.

Chapter 1

Nate looked up from a blueprint he was inspecting when he heard a soft knock.

"Enter."

A wisp of a woman slipped inside. She was wearing a dull brown frock and her hair was tucked neatly under a cap. "Good morning, your grace. I am Miss Fiona Butterworth."

Nate signalled her to take a seat, subjecting her to the full force of his dukishness.

She curtseyed gracefully and sat on his leatherback chair, not seeming very intimidated.

Nate noticed that although she was plain, her black eyes were frank. And she looked younger than he'd expected. Redgrave had said that she'd worked with them for five years...

"How old are you, Miss Butterworth, if you don't mind my asking?"

"I do not mind, your grace. I am two and twenty."

Nate couldn't keep the surprise from his face. He held back a retort. Why the hell had Redgrave even hired her when she'd been what...seventeen? Did he have a fetish for young girls that Nate hadn't heard of?

He examined the girl again.

She was definitely not a diamond of the first water—not by any stretch. But he conceded that although she was on the slimmer side, she had a surprisingly nice figure. Her face was pleasant as well.

Yes, maybe Redgrave had employed her for other reasons. What had been wrong with him? Why had he taken advise from Redgrave of all people? Oh yes, he'd been desperate.

"Miss Butterworth, I'm afraid I cannot employ you."

It was a shame, really.

"Why?" she stood up, aghast.

"I do not think you're in any position to question me," he replied haughtily.

He saw her face contort with anger before she closed her eyes and counted to ten. Audibly.

Nate didn't know if he should be appalled or amused.

"Your grace, with all due respect," she practically spat the words, "I would merely like to know why you wouldn't hire me."

He stared at her. He didn't owe her any explanation. And he certainly couldn't tell her what he thought about her—not directly.

She didn't seem cowed in the least. If anything, her spine straightened a bit more and her eyes flashed with indignation.

Nate felt a spark of admiration but he didn't dare show it.

"Since you ask so nicely," he paused to see if she noticed his sarcasm. She had, if her clenched jaw was any indication. He bit back a smile and continued, "I do not wish to hire you because I believe you do not have enough experience."

"What?! I have been a companion—and a very good one at that—for the last five years."

"Yes, but you are so very young."

"Age is just a number," she said dismissively.

"Alright," he conceded. She didn't look like she was going to let this go because she was standing before him with her hand on her hips, tapping her foot impatiently as she waited for him to go on. Yes, she was going to make him say it.

Nate cleared his throat. "I know why Redgrave hired you."

"Yes, because I'm dam— very good at what I do."

"And what exactly do you do?"

"I act as a companion, of course," she replied, as if he was daft.

It was Nate's turn to count till ten.

"I do not require the sort of services from you that Redgrave did," he finally said.

She was chewing her lip in a distracted manner and that was distracting him.

"Are you quite alright, you grace?" she came close to him and touched his forehead.

"What are you doing?" He sputtered angrily. Her breasts were practically brushing against his face. She jumped back.

"I was just checking," she said a little defensively. "Can I be blunt?"

"I wasn't aware that you were being circumspect until now," he muttered.

She went on as if she hadn't heard him. "Yes, well. You see, your grace, you aren't making a lot of sense."

Nate had to gape at that.

"It would be more agreeable if you could just tell me—clearly—what the problem here is," she said slowly, as if speaking to a child.

Nate counted to twenty this time.

"Miss Butterworth, can I be blunt?"

"Oh please do!"

"I do not wish to bed you."

"Wha—"

Nate put up his hand, interrupting her. "It's nothing personal, I assure you. You're perfectly lovely. But I want someone who would only be a companion to my mother."

Nate noticed that her face had turned a peculiar shade of red. He supposed she hadn't taken his rejection well. He opened his mouth to apologise but she beat him to it.

"Now listen here, your grace. I am not a loose woman. I am only a companion. And if I were a man, I would've called you out for suggesting otherwise," she said angrily.

She looked like she was telling the truth. Nate blinked.

Of course she wasn't a loose woman. She had virtuous written all over her face. In bold letters at that.

He felt like a thousand kinds of fool for jumping to such conclusions.

What had he been thinking? He supposed he should apologise but he was a bloody Duke.

"You must know how Redgrave is. So it was only natural for me to conclude that—"

"Natural? I think not."

But when she saw the embarrassment on his face, her face softened. Just a little.

"The Baron was handsy. But I managed to resist his advances. I repeat, I was only a companion."

Nate sighed and rubbed his temples. He'd really blundered this time.

"What can I do to make it up to you for this transgression?"

"Allow me to act as your mother's companion?"

"Miss Butterworth, I still think that you're too young—"

"Your grace, I am most certainly not."

"You are too young for her to enjoy your company and too feeble to help her physically. I am looking for someone sturd—"

"Oh alright just give me a fortnight and I'll prove it to you. If you still don't want me after that, I shall leave gracefully."

Oh but the woman drove a hard bargain.

"Two weeks it is. You can start tomorrow," he sighed defeatedly.

"You won't want me to leave, you'll see!" she grinned before dipping into a clumsy curtsey and toppling a sculpture placed on a stand near the door in her haste to leave.

"I hope that wasn't very dear," she choked out.

It was.

"I'll clean in up right away!"

"No. Just let it be, I shall call for someone else to do it."

"I'll be on my way then," she inched closer to the door, not liking his thunderous expression.

Good.

"Go."

And then she was gone.

Nate strangely felt like he'd been swallowed up by a tornado and then spit out.

He took out his pocket watch and saw that she'd been here for a mere ten minutes.

And he was already exhausted.

He thought she was extremely unprofessional and young and a terrible choice. In fact, he'd had every intention of sending her on her way as soon as he'd heard her age. Something told him that this Butterworth woman was bad news. And he usually heeded to his instincts.

But here he was, saddled with his mother's new companion. If only for two weeks.

And Nate suspected this was going to be the longest fortnight of his life.

Chapter 2

"Mother, may I enter?" Nate knocked on her door.

"You may not, Nathaniel."

Nate rolled his eyes and pushed open the door.

"Why haven't you taken your supper yet?"

"I am not hungry."

"Mother..."

"I do not wish to speak with you."

"Why not?"

"Because you hired that damned woman!"

Of course, Winterbottom had told her.

Nate sighed and sat beside her on the bed. He took her wrinkled hand in his. She tried to pull it away but he didn't loosen his grip.

"Look at me," he cajoled.

She grunted and finally turned to look at him.

"I am only concerned about you," he said sincerely.

Her face softened. "Your concern is misplaced. A companion is not what I need."

"Then what is it? What do you need?"

She opened her mouth but then swallowed back her retort.

"It's nothing."

"Do this for me. Give her a chance. If you don't like her after two weeks, we'll send her away."

"I'm confident that I won't like her after her first day here."

"But I have already paid her the wages for the first two weeks. We can't let all that money go to waste, now can we?"

"Of course not. I'll make her work, you count on it," his mother huffed. Nate laughed and nodded, not sure if he should feel sorry for Miss Butterworth or his mother.

"Does your leg still hurt?"

"It's better now that you're here," she smiled.

Nate squeezed her hand.

He didn't know what to say. He loved his mother, but ever since his father had passed a few years back, he had become busy with his new responsibilities and he hadn't been there for his mother. They had drifted apart and now Nate didn't know if he could bridge the distance even he tried.

He knew he spent more time in London than he needed to. But he preferred it that way.

Besides, it would only be this way for a few more months. Then he'd get married to Sophia and his mother wouldn't be lonely again.

Although she wasn't very pleased with his choice for a wife, Nate didn't fret about it. He knew his mother would never find any woman good enough for him. And he would be thirty in a year, it was imperative that he married and produced heirs while he was still in his prime.

Besides, Sophia was perfect. She was beautiful—a diamond of the first water—unlike that Butterworth woman. And she was polished and poised—not clumsy like the woman he'd encountered that morning. And most of all, she was the daughter of a Duke. She deserved to be his duchess. She didn't make his pulse quicken with desire but at least she wouldn't embarrass him—unlike Butterworth.

Why was he even thinking about his mother's temporary companion, he thought.

The woman was trouble and he was overwrought—that was it.

"Will you eat now?"

His mother nodded.

"Good. Good night, mother," he kissed her cheek.

"Good night, Nathaniel," she replied but Nate didn't miss the disappointment on her face.

He merely nodded awkwardly and turned around to leave.

****

"How's the bread, nana? I added some special herbs in the dough," Fiona asked her nana as she settled onto the creaking chair of their small dining table.

"It's alright," she huffed.

"You're still angry about this morning?"

"Yes."

"Nana! I wasn't hungry."

"You didn't eat because you knew there'd be no food left for me if you did," her nana retorted shrewdly.

Fiona's cheeks reddened with embarrassment.

"It's alright now. I got two week's wages in advance. I hardly know how to spend it all," she said cheerfully. Nana rolled her eyes but let it go.

"I forgot to ask. How was the Duke? Was he very handsome?"

Fiona began to cough.

"Here," Nana offered her a glass of water. "Are you alright?"

Fiona nodded, her eyes watering from coughing too much.

How was she to explain to Nana what the Duke looked like? How was she to tell that she'd never seen a man more handsome?

Fiona had never seen eyes that beautiful shade of blue. And she'd never seen such lips on a man—wide and firm. With his black hair and straight nose, he'd looked positively sinful.

And so Fiona changed the topic because there was no way in hell that she could explain to her Nana that for the first time in her life, she'd been affected by someone. Not by his title and certainly not by his less than gentlemanly behaviour, but by his presence—his personality. He exuded...something. And so she'd found herself tongue tied.

Anyhow, the Duke only had his looks to recommend him, she consoled herself.

She'd had half a mind to stomp out of ridiculously gorgeous man's house and never look back. But she'd swallowed her pride and decided to stay.

Not that he wanted you to, her conscience whispered.

Well, she'd needed the money.

She'd been the sole earning member in her family ever since her parents had passed away when she'd been fifteen. Her father had been a vicar and had had few savings.

They'd managed to scrape by—Nana and her—for a few years. But then it had become imperative that she work. Nana was too old to do anything. She hated watching Fiona work but they had no other choice and she knew that.

And so, this wasn't the first time Fiona found herself swallowing her pride.

But she was happy. And she was grateful.

Chapter 3

"You are late, Miss Butterworth," the butler said to her, looking down his long nose at her.

"I most certainly am not," Fiona burst out, wagging her finger before his equally long face.

"What is all this commotion about?" the Duke appeared out of no where.

"This woman, you grace," the butler began indignantly, "is late. And she refuses to accept it."

"I arrived on time, your grace. Your butler is simply being a boor," Fiona retorted.

"I never—" he began but the Duke held up his hand.

The Duke closed his eyes as if in pain. And then, "Winterbottom, I asked her to come at half past nine. And she is on time."

"But all the other servants report at nine, your grace," Winterbottom sniffed delicately.

"Yes. But Miss Butterworth isn't a servant—she's a companion. To my mother. And since mother wakes only at ten, I asked to come at half past nine," the Duke explained patiently.

"Alright then, your grace," the butler said looking close to tears. With one last disdainful glance at Fiona, he stomped off.

"I think you need a new butler," Fiona said to the Duke.

"Winterbottom has been serving our family for the last thirty years, Miss Butterworth. So no, we do not need a new butler," the Duke replied coldly.

Fiona held up her hands in surrender. "It was a joke."

"I would appreciate it if you would attend to my mother now," he replied before walking away and disappearing into what she'd discovered yesterday was his study.

"Where is the duchess?" she asked no one in particular. She was standing all alone by the entrance of the grotesquely large hall, not knowing where to go.

You have made a mistake by coming here, her conscience whispered. Fiona didn't necessarily disagree with her. But it was too late now...

She tentatively navigated the house and asked a few friendly servants where she could find the duchess. And then she found herself standing outside her rooms.

Fiona raised her hand and knocked twice.

"Come in," she heard a heavy voice from the other side.

She pushed open the heavy door and went in.

There she was, the dowager duchess, laying on her bed.

"Who are you?" she questioned, taking in Fiona's appearance.

"I am your new companion, your grace," she curtseyed.

"Hmph."

"Your grace?"

"I don't really need your services girl, I said so to my son. But he was adamant, so I relented. I suggest you enjoy your time here and make use of the kitchens or roam the gardens—do anything you wish. Just don't bother me."

Fiona looked on with wide eyes. She didn't know what to say.

This woman clearly needed a companion—the Duke was right. She was just far too lonely and far too proud to admit it.

Fiona had two options—she could either get cowed by her grace's lofty title and just listen to her or she could show her that she was made of sterner stuff and do her duty.

The former was the easier thing to do, of course. But Fiona had never been one to walk away from a challenge.

She dragged in a deep breath.

"With all due respect, your grace, as kind as your offer is, I'm afraid I must decline. I came here with the sole intention of acting as your companion and fulfilling all your needs. And nothing—not even you shall keep me from doing my duty," she said.

The duchess just stared at her, her mouth opening and closing like a fish.

And then she heard her response. It was so soft that Fiona almost missed it.

"Very well."

"Really?" Fiona grinned.

"Fetch me my breakfast. Make sure you bring it and no one else."

"Right away, your grace," Fiona nodded and left the chamber.

This was good, wasn't it? Although she didn't seem very enthusiastic, at least she was giving Fiona something to do.

She happily skipped her way to the kitchens—again, after asking for directions.

"Hullo everyone. I'm Miss Fiona Butterworth and I am her grace's new companion," she announced as she entered the hot kitchens.

"Oh we all know who you are," one of the scullery maids smiled.

"You do? How?" she asked, perplexed.

"Well, you stood up to Winterbottom. That ought to make you popular," a portly man chortled.

"He's a bully is what he is," another maid complained.

"Now that's a stretch. He's just overprotective and a little possessive about the Duke and his family," the portly man admonished lightly. The maid merely rolled her eyes and turned to her dishes.

"Thank you for the warm welcome, I guess. I'm looking forward to getting to know all of you better but later," Fiona smiled. "Her grace wished to break her fast if it's ready."

"It is. We shall send it up immediately," the cook nodded.

"No, I will take it."

"Miss Butterworth, I'll send it with our footman Tom."

"But Her grace specially asked me to bring it."

All the servants turned to look at each other's faces in confusion.

"What is it?" Fiona spoke up.

"There is no way you can carry the tray all the way to her chambers, my dear. It is too heavy for a girl like you to carry it."

Oh.

So it looked like her grace had other plans for her.

Very well.

"I can and I will," Fiona winked at the troubled servants.

Chapter 4

"Thank you, Radcliffe. You make leave now," Nate nodded at his solicitor.

"Your grace," the man bowed before exiting his study. "Send for me once you've read all the papers."

As soon as he heard the sound of the door clicking shut, Nate pushed all the paperwork on his desk with a swish of his hand.

Lord, but being a Duke was exhausting. And dull. Not at all as glamorous as people thought it to be.

He let his head fall into his hands and let out a weary sigh.

Just then he heard a knock.

Must be Winterbottom.

Good, the butler would help him pick up all the important paperwork that he'd just dumped on the floor heedlessly.

"Your grace, may I enter?" came a female voice with another set of impatient knocks.

That most certainly wasn't Winterbottom.

"Just a moment," he called and quickly crouched to the floor to pick up all the papers. It wouldn't do if Miss Butterworth witnessed his study in such a mess—he was a dignified Duke after all.

"Is everything alright?" came her muffled voice.

"Yes. I just need a moment," he ground out.

"Are you sure? Because I can help if—"

"I said everything is fine," he thundered, cutting off whatever she was about to say.

"Alright then."

Oh but the woman was talkative.

And what did she need from him anyway? Did she want to quit already—hadn't it only been four days? He'd heard about what his mother had been doing–making her lift heavy trays and the like. He'd thought about berating his mother for it but he'd thought better of it. The sooner Miss Butterworth left, the better.

Where was the other paper?

He looked frantically about his desk, on all fours now.

"Ah," he murmured as he spotted it stuck beneath the leg of his desk.

He pulled at it but it didn't budge.

How did it even get stuck there?!

He pulled again with a loud grunt.

It moved a little but the door opened as well and he turned to find Miss Butterworth standing at the doorway, staring rather shamelessly at his posterior.

Fiona swallowed.

The Duke sure had a fine pair of buttcheeks, she thought to herself.

Then again, there wasn't one thing about him that wasn't fine—she thought more than a little disgruntled.

"I believe I asked you to wait, Miss Butterworth," his voice was cold as ice as he hastily got up from the floor and dusted his clothes.

Fiona resisted the urge to giggle.

"Yes, well—I heard sounds and I thought you might need a hand," she said defensively when he continued to stare at her.

What was he doing beneath his desk on his knees anyway?

He muttered something(uncomplimentary, no doubt) under his breath before taking a seat behind his desk.

"How can I help you, Miss Butterworth? Have you decided to quit already?" his voice held just a hint of condescension which was enough to set her on the edge.

"Now look here, your grace, I am no quitter. I merely came here to request you to restock your library," Fiona huffed.

"What is wrong with my library?" He looked appalled.

"Many things. Firstly, the books are impossible to reach. The shelves are too high for practicality. Secondly, your collection of books are awful—"

"Our library here is stocked with the books written by every renowned writer of the last four centuries," he replied, his jaw tighter than she would've liked.

"Yes, but that is exactly my point. You haven't updated it at all."

The Duke just raised one brow, silently asking her to continue.

"There's no new content. Her grace has already read almost all the books. And the variety is limited as well."

"Very well, I shall order a new collection immediately. Anything else?" he asked, his blue eyes impatient.

"No, your grace," Fiona grinned.

"Very well," he said and bent to the papers on his desk, the dismissal clear.

Fiona shrugged and turned to leave. And then, "there is something else," she turned about.

"The Duke looked heavenward before looking at her. "Yes, Miss Butterworth?"

"Make sure you order a lot of romance novels. You know the kind where—"

"I am sure that my mother does not read romance novels—especially not at her age."

"Yes but she could. Romance is so much better than reading about how to manage agricultural lands or some dead man's life history or philosophy. Philosophy is just plain dull and—"

"I get your drift," he interrupted her. "I shall order romance novels as well. Just leave a list."

"Thank you, your grace," Fiona curtseyed and rushed outside the door.

Little did she know that when she shut the door behind her with a loud thud, the brand new Ming vase placed on the little table next to the door fell to the ground and broke in two.

Little did she know that Duke silently cursed her for it.

And little did she know that the Duke was close to pulling his hair out and losing his mind.

Off she went, blissful in her ignorance.

****

Hey guys, hope all of you are doing well. I also hope that you're enjoying the book. Like always, I'm dying to hear from you so please comment and don't forget to vote and show your support.

Love,Ashmita

Chapter 5

"Fiona, please stop singing—or whatever it is that you're doing," Nana groaned, walking about their small cottage on wobbly legs, the tap tap sound of her walking stick against the wooden floor punctuating her words.

"Why?" she asked, halting her song midway while her hands still worked as she put in some fresh bread into her lunch basket.

"Because my poor ears may start bleeding at any given moment."

"You're just exaggerating nana. I might not be the best of singers but I do have a pleasing voice—Lady Henrietta would say so often."

"Your Lady Henrietta was deaf. You told me so yourself," Nana rolled her eyes.

Fiona huffed before beginning to sing again.

She'd got out two words when Nana interrupted again.

"Don't you have to leave?"

"I do."

"Then leave."

"Oh alright. I'm sure the birds and the rabbits in the woods would enjoy my singing," she muttered as she took off.

"I highly doubt that, but whatever makes you happy."

Fiona pretended she didn't hear her, the way she usually did.

She strolled through the woods leisurely, singing all the while—no nana to interrupt her song this time.

But still, her brain whirred. She thought about how she could get the duchess to like her more. The old tyrant had softened a little—Fiona had sensed it. She didn't even demand that Fiona carry her trays of food any more.

But if she had to stay longer, she'd have to do better. And as much as she hated to admit it, she had taken a liking to the dowager duchess. There was something about her gruff manner that Fiona found endearing. It reminded her of her Nana Jeanette.

Not to mention, the Duke has caught her interest as well.

More than once he'd caught him checking on his mother. She'd seen the way he treated all the servants. Although he was gruff—a bit like his mother and grumpy, he was kind.

Except to her.

He wasn't unkind, per say. It was more that he couldn't tolerate her and wanted to be rid of her. Why else would he have heeded to Fiona's request for more books so quickly?

She sighed.

Why was she even thinking about the Duke? He was way out of her league and besides, he was betrothed. The house keeper had said so herself.

And although Fiona wasn't romantically inclined towards the duke, she couldn't help but feel just a teeny weeny bit of jealousy for the Lady he was to marry. She was a Duke's daughter, she'd heard. His equal in every way.

When she reached the Duke's estate, she removed her coat. She was surprised when Winterbottom took it from her hand—as if he wasn't quite sure why he was helping her.

Looks like the butler had softened towards her too, Fiona thought with a smug grin.

"The Duke requested your presence in the receiving parlour, Miss Butterworth," he informed her.

What now? Her two weeks weren't up yet. Was he dismissing her already?

Over her dead body.

Fiona stomped her way in the direction of the parlour. She knocked impatiently and waited for his permission to enter.

The Duke was seated on a plush sofa, a cup of tea in his hands. He looked almost relaxed. She'd only ever seen him with his head stuck in a heap of papers in his study.

My, but he was a handsome devil, she thought grudgingly. The curtains were pulled aside, allowing the sunlight to stream into the room. It glinted off his dark hair. And his skin looked smooth and tanned—as if he spent a lot of time outdoors.

"Good morning, Miss Butterworth," he said and motioned for her to enter. Goodness gracious, even his voice was perfect.

"Good morning, your grace," she smiled slightly. "You wished to see me?"

"Yes. Please take a seat."

Fiona sat as demurely as she was capable of on a small arm chair opposite to him.

"Take some tea."

"No, thank you, your grace. It wouldn't be proper."

"I insist, Miss Butterworth," he said simply, his eyes taking that commanding look again. She complied. If she could put up with Baron Redgrave trying to get under her skirts, she could certainly handle a high handed duke.

"I'd like to talk about my mother."

"What is it, your grace? Is she unhappy with me? Have I made some mistake?"

"Not at all. I merely wished to hear from you about the progress you've made with her so far."

"Well, I can see that she still doesn't want a companion. But she seems to have taken a liking towards me. She even asked me to accompany her on her evening stroll the other day. And she asked me if the books had arrived."

"They have, as a matter of fact."

"Oh already?" Fiona clapped her hands in glee, her lips stretching in a wide smile.

But the Duke merely stared at her.

"Your grace?"

"Hmm?" he blinked.

"Oh never mind," she chuckled and stood up. "May I go to Her grace now? It is time for her breakfast."

He merely nodded.

Fiona curtseyed and left.

Chapter 6

"What would you like to do now, your grace?" Fiona asked the Duchess who was reclining on her bed after taking her luncheon. "Shall I fetch the new books? Maybe I can read to you from one of them?"

"I want to rest my eyes for a bit."

"Oh alright," Fiona replied, unable to hide the disappointment from her face.

"You go on. Find me something you think I'd enjoy and bring it up. You can read to me once I've risen."

Fiona opened her mouth to add something but then shut her mouth.

"You can read while I sleep."

Fiona resisted the urge to squeal her delight and curtseyed quickly before rushing out of the bed chamber.

She skipped her way down the stairs before running in the direction of the library.

She only had to look for a few minutes before she spotted the new leather bound books.

Only, they were placed on the high shelf, impossible for her to reach.

That was odd.

Fiona dragged the ladder to the shelf and climbed up without further ado. She'd piled about six novels in her arms when she heard the Duke's enraged voice.

"What in God's name are you doing, woman?"

"Picking out some novels," she replied cheerfully.

"I can see that," he ground out. "I'm asking you why you're ten feet above the ground when you can trip on your skirts, fall and break your neck."

"I'm fine, your grace. You worry needlessly. I climb ladders like these in my skirts all the time," she said distractedly as she picked out another book.

The Duke muttered something under his breath.

Fiona paid him no mind. She was too excited right now to let his surliness bother her.

He moved across the room and stood next to her ladder, hands on his hips.

Fiona looked down at him.

He looked like a worried mother hen. She stifled a giggle.

"Hand me the books."

Fiona obeyed.

"Now get down. Carefully."

She huffed.

Did the man think he was God?!

She began to descend one step at a time, muttering her displeasure all the while. And then she tripped.

Of course she tripped—the Duke had willed it after all.

And of course the Duke caught her, being the gentleman that he was.

Fiona closed her eyes, humiliated.

When Miss Butterworth finally opened her eyes, Nate found himself at a loss of words.

He meant to berate her, to scold her for being so careless. He opened his mouth to form the words, but he discovered that talking was difficult when one couldn't breathe.

And that was what he felt—as if the breath had whooshed out of him. Not because she was heavy, she was light as a feather—such a tiny thing.

Her eyes were wide and her lips had parted in the most delightful way. Her body was warm and supple in his arms. And her hands clutched the front of his coat trustingly.

Nate wanted to bend down and capture her lush lips in a kiss. He wanted to taste her sweetness—the need to do so too great.

What the hell was he thinking?!

Nate dropped her without thought, as if she'd burnt him.

She fell to the carpeted floor with an ooff and looked up at him accusingly.

"What did you catch me when you had to drop me again anyway?" she muttered, struggling to get on her feet.

Nate felt a smile tug at his mouth but he kept it in a firm line.

"I told you to be careful."

"Yes, well...you were just standing there and I got nervous! And the books were placed so high," she replied, her brown hair falling from her simple bun.

Nate didn't know what devil had prompted him to order Winterbottom to put the books as high as possible but he'd eat his hessians before he admitted as much to her.

"So it was my fault then..." the statement rhetorical but she chose to reply with an indignant "Yes."

Nate was too surprised by her audacity to say anything.

She bent and picked up all the books that he'd dropped in his haste to catch her.

She turned about and left then without saying anything to him.

Nate sat on a chair placed there with a thud.

Again, he felt exhausted. Drained.

He needed some whiskey. Badly.

He couldn't believe he'd almost kissed that Butterworth woman. He couldn't believe that he wanted to hold her to him, that he'd wanted her closer to him than she'd been.

She was bewitching him. Yes. The woman was a witch—that had to be it.

Because this morning, when she'd smiled at him in his receiving chamber, he'd been similarly lost. He'd not heard what she'd said and neither had he remembered that she was his mother's companion.

He'd thought that she was lovely—a breath of fresh air.

But he hadn't read too much into it. He'd ignored his momentary lapse. Nate couldn't very well ignore what had transpired just now.

Especially because he knew that it hadn't been one sided. He'd seen the spark of awareness in her eyes—mirroring his.

The woman was his mother's companion, beneath him in rank and breeding. And he was betrothed, god damnit.

He was just over wrought, Nate told himself. He took a deep breath.

Why was he overreacting?

So he'd discovered that Miss Butterworth was a lovely young woman. So he'd wanted her for that brief moment.

That didn't mean he was suddenly taken with her.

The thought of the improper, loud and highly opinionated Miss Butterworth as anything more than his mother's companion made him balk.

That was a good sign, wasn't it?

Chapter 7

"You seem distracted, Fiona," the duchess observed.

"Not at all, your grace. Why do you say so?" Fiona stuttered.

"Because you've read the same paragraph three times."

Oh.

She was distracted, alright. Completely lost.

And it was that damned Duke's fault.

He'd looked at her like that. And held her like that. And nobody had ever looked or held her like that before today.

But that wasn't the worst part.

The worst part was that she'd looked back at him like that too. And she'd certainly not been in a hurry to get out of his arms.

Yes.

That was where the problem lay.

Fiona Butterworth was infatuated.

Wasn't that what this was? She hadn't stopped thinking about him ever since she'd quit his study.

No man had ever caught her fancy, not even the dear Mr. Johnson. He was the new vicar, handsome and young. He'd also expressed his interest in her—more than once. And he was perfect, her equal—the way the Duke's Lady was his equal. But Fiona had never been able to see him as anything other than a good friend.

So why did she have to go and get infatuated with a Duke? A betrothed, surly Duke, no less.

"Is something amiss?" the Duchess interrupted her thoughts.

"No, your grace. I'm just touched by how much the hero loves his lady," she tried to smile. "And that was a particularly interesting paragraph."

"Hmph. Go on then."

Fiona read on, making sure her mind didn't wander this time.

"How did you like it so far, your grace?"

"It's pathetic. I refuse to believe that my son selected this book. The writing is horrible and the plot is simply atrocious. How many times can that Rebecca girl possibly swoon?!"

There was no way she was telling the duchess that she'd chosen the book herself now.

Still, she strongly disagreed with the duchess. Maybe it was a little too clichéd, but it was certainly entertaining.

Besides, she'd seen the old crone hang on to every word that Fiona had read. She could pretend to be intellectual all she liked, but it seemed she liked some drama and romance just like Fiona. She stifled a grin.

"Do you wish for me to read you another book perhaps, your grace?"

"No!"

Fiona raised her brows.

"It's just that I don't like to leave any book unfinished," she replied, her cheeks reddening a bit.

Oh sure.

"Go on, now. It is growing late."

"Alright, your grace. I shall see you tomorrow morn," Fiona got up and curtseyed. She left the book on the table next to her bed, just in case.

On her way out, she had to cross the Duke's study and she found herself slowing down. She looked that way even though the door was shut.

Good God, she was in trouble.

Who was she going to tell this to? Who could possibly guide her through this disaster?

And then it struck her—there was only one person she could count on.

Fiona raced back home.

"Nana!" she hollered.

"What is it, girl?" Nana's voice was laced with panic as she exited her room.

"I need your help."

"Is something amiss?"

"Yes. No."

"Yes or no?" Nana asked impatiently.

"I don't know," Fiona groaned, chucking her basket onto their small dining table.

Nana rolled her eyes before looking heavenward.

"Sit down first."

Fiona complied, making herself comfortable on their threadbare sofa. Nana settled down on her arm chair.

"Now tell me what happened."

"I think I'm infatuated."

"With?"

"The Duke."

Nana muttered something under her breath. Fiona didn't know what she said but Nana didn't look particularly optimistic.

"What do I do, Nana? I'm doomed!" she wailed.

"Stop being so dramatic, Fiona. You're only infatuated, not in love. So we can repair the damage." And then she added an "if you want to," as an afterthought.

"Of course I want to. Why wouldn't I want to?!"

"Well, if something could come out of this, I see no harm in you following your heart and—"

"Nothing can ever come out of this, I assure you."

"Why ever not?"

"Are you out of your mind, Nana? He's a Duke. And he's betrothed."

"Not married. And handsome," Nana smirked.

"Nana! Are you going to help me or not?"

"Oh alright," she huffed. "How did it all start though?"

Fiona briefed her about what had taken place in the library and about how she'd witnessed his kindness.

"I think I'm infatuated, myself," Nana grinned.

Fiona resisted the urge to strangle her great-grandmother.

"I don't really know what we can do about this, Fiona. You cannot possible ignore him, he lives there, after all. And you can't pursue him—although I don't necessarily agree. So what is it that we can do?"

"I asked you because I didn't know," Fiona ground out.

"I'm hungry."

"Nana?"

"What?! I need time to think. We shall sup and then I'll think," she huffed and got up.

Fiona wanted to scream. But she dutifully got up and readied a simple dinner.

She ate in silence. A million thoughts formed in her head and each one was about the damned Duke.

She didn't even like him.

Nana promptly dozed off after supper and Fiona wasn't even surprised. She went to bed, unaware of what the next morning would bring her.

Chapter 8

It was a pleasant afternoon, Fiona thought to herself with a soft smile as she made her way into the maze.

The duchess had shooed her away from the gardens saying she intended to nap outdoors.

The woman could sleep anywhere. Much like her nana.

Anyhow, Fiona wasn't pleased about the reprieve today. She didn't need more time on her hands—that would only lead to her traitorous thoughts about the Duke return to her head. She'd banished them with great difficulty by keeping herself occupied at all times. And keeping her distance from him the way she would from the plague.

"Oh wonderful," she muttered to herself. She was lost now. Lost, distracted and infatuated with the wrong man.

She stopped short.

She was being ridiculous was what it was. And she was obviously overreacting. Tons of people got infatuated all the time, it was perfectly normal. Even Jimmy the stable boy was infatuated with Lily the downstairs maid, wasn't he?

Except, he could do something about his feelings, unlike you, her subconscious chided her.

This was too much negativity for her.

Fiona cleared her throat, she'd sing. Singing always made her feel better. She knew it was probably silly for her to break into a song at the drop of a hat at every inconvenience—much like the troubled heroine of the novel she'd been reading to the duchess. But there was no one here to see or hear...

Nate was going in search of his mother when a familiar sound reached his ears. He stopped walking.

Was it a figment of his imagination?

It had to be. Because it sounded exactly like the song he'd heard in the woods the other day. That voice...that terrible voice—surely it couldn't be.

He moved closer to the maze, where the sounds seemed to be emerging from.

He followed the sound this time, loathe to ignore it again. He smoothly made his way towards the centre, where the sounds became louder, the words clearer.

By now he was certainly was the same woman he'd heard in the woods. There was no mistaking that voice...

And then he saw her or her back as she sat on a bench at the centre facing away from him.

But there was no mistaking whose back that was or whose voice now.

"It was you, all this time."

She stood up in a flash and turned around, her song coming to an abrupt halt.

"I beg your pardon?" she asked breathlessly, her eyes wide and her cheeks beginning to colour. He moved towards her and then sat down on the bench.

"I heard you sing in the woods that morning...it was you, wasn't it? Singing this very song?" he laughed, he couldn't help it.

She looked at him as if he'd sprouted horns but then nodded slowly. When he didn't stop laughing, her lips pursed in disapproval.

"I fail to see what is so amusing."

"You're voice," he whooped. "No offence," he added, still laughing.

Hell, he couldn't stop his laughter. He should've known that it would be her. No other woman could sing so terribly and confidently at the same time.

Soon the pinched expression left her face and she joined his laughter sheepishly.

"Come now, your grace, surely I don't sound that bad," she laughed.

"Oh you have no idea, sweetheart," he grinned. Nate didn't remember the last time he'd laughed so much or so freely. He had Miss Butterworth to thank just now.

Too late he realised that he'd called her sweetheart and that Miss Butterworth had ceased laughing. He stopped laughing too. The sight of her arresting him.

This close, he could see her chocolatey eyes shine with something he didn't wish to dwell on. Freckles dusted her nose. And her mouth, a healthy pink, reminded him of strawberries.

A longing so strong assailed him that he was momentarily paralysed.

It was just that she was so real, her innate beauty shining from within. He'd been an idiot to think she was plain.

Just one taste. One taste and he'd leave her be.

He bent closer to her slowly, giving her time to draw back and slap him for his impudence, half hoping she would do it and put an end to this madness.

But of course Miss Butterworth didn't do what he expected her to. Instead, she inched closer too, her face merely an inch away from his, her breathing shallow. She closed her eyes and tilted her head up.

The invitation was too hard to resist and Nate was no saint. So he bent down and took her lips in a searing kiss before she could change her mind.

And what a kiss.

Miss Butterworth had no idea of what to do and so she was still. But not stiff, oh no. Nate didn't remove his mouth from hers even to breathe. He fed on the softness of her, holding her face between his palms even as her hands came around his neck.

Nate groaned.

Heavens above, but she was sweet. So very sweet and Nate burned for her.

It occurred to him that when she wasn't arguing with him or challenging his servants or breaking his vases, Fiona Butterworth was a bloody fine woman.

He released her mouth so they could breathe and made to resume their kiss but just as he leaned into her, she stiffened, as if realising only now what they'd done.

She pushed him and stood up, her cheeks red with embarrassment.

Here we go.

"Miss Butterworth—"

But she held up her hand. "I'm so sorry, your grace. I shouldn't have done that."

Nate's mouth dropped open. What the hell was she talking about. He'd kissed her like a rouge and she was taking responsibility for what happened?

"Miss—"

"And I don't want you to think that I behave this way with all of my employers—I've never before done such a thing. Please don't dismiss me," she pleaded, sounding panicky.

Good God, he was an ass.

"Miss Butterworth, I initiated that kiss and you have nothing to apologise for. If anyone should, it is I. I don't know what came over me..." he sighed.

"So you won't dismiss me?"

"No!"

She smiled then. Albeit hesitantly.

"You shouldn't apologise, your grace. I enjoyed it."

Why did she have to be so honest?! Nate closed his eyes. He was still hard from their kissing and she had to entice him this way?

"I shall not repeat this."

"Of course I understand that, your grace," she replied wide eyed.

Nate stood up, hoping the evidence of his desire wasn't very prominent.

"Will you make your way out on your own?"

"I did come inside on my own, didn't I?" she smirked, back to being her annoying self.

Nate muttered a few curses under his breath and left without a backward glance.

Chapter 9

Once she was sure that the Duke had left, Fiona landed on the bench on her bottom.

Clearly this had been a mistake. A very large—enormous error of judgement on both their parts. And she was just as responsible for it as the Duke.

Fiona had never been kissed before and she'd never felt like kissing anyone either. But when the Duke had bent closer—just a little, she'd wanted to kiss him. She'd laughed with him...and what a lovely laugh he had—it had made her feel special.

He kissed the way he seemed to do everything else...passionately, thoroughly and sincerely. The mere touch of his lips against hers had made her want to climb atop his lap and never leave.

He'd kissed her and he'd whispered her name. And he'd called her Fiona, not Miss Butterworth the way he usually did.

That had to mean something, didn't it?

Hope unfurled in her bosom but she squelched it ruthlessly.

He'd said that this wouldn't happen again which meant he didn't want this to turn into anything more.

It meant that he'd kissed her and then remembered that he had a fiancé waiting for him. And he'd never jilt the daughter of a Duke for the impoverished one of a deceased vicar.

And he was probably in love with his Lady.

That thought brought a swift stab of pain. The pain brought on tears she hadn't known she'd been holding.

Fiona furiously wiped the dampness off her cheeks.

She had brought this upon herself, she chided herself. She had made the mistake of imagining a romance where there had never been scope for one.

She got up and slowly made her way outside the maze. Outside, she found the duchess awake, sipping tea.

"I apologise for being gone so long, your grace. I got lost in the maze."

"It's alright, people often get lost in there," the duchess eyed her shrewdly.

Fiona was positive the Duke hadn't told his mother of what had happened in there but the knowing way she was looking at her...

Oh she was being silly.

"It has grown windy, shall we go inside now?" Fiona asked, fussing with the Duchess's shawl.

"Yes."

Fiona was solemn the rest of the evening. And if the duchess noted her pensive mood, she made no comment on it.

Soon it began to rain and Fiona had to wait for it to let until she could leave. The duchess offered her carriage of course, but Fiona had declined. She didn't want to take any unnecessary favours.

And then it had grown too dark.

"I cannot possibly in good conscience let you go alone now!"

"I'll be fine, your grace. You worry needlessly."

"No, my decision is final. You cannot even take a carriage now, the roads are completely ruined and it would be foolish to risk travelling that path. You will simply have to stay here tonight. I shall ask Miss Perkins to prepare a room for you."

"But—"

"It is an order." The Duchess's expression was haughty, making Fiona swallow her protests.

"Then I do not really have a choice, do I?" Fiona grumbled and settled into her chair.

"Not one," she smiled smugly. "What about your grandmother? Will she be alright?"

"Oh yes. Nana Jeanette is used to it because my previous employer was very sickly towards the end and I would often stay the night with her. And she's my great grandmother," Fiona grinned.

The duchess raised her eyebrows at that but didn't comment.

"Are you ready to take your supper, your grace?"

"Yes. You will eat with me as well."

"As you wish," Fiona smiled and stood up to ring for a maid. It pleased her immensely that the woman was growing more comfortable with her. And not just because that meant she could keep her position as her companion. About that though...

"Why aren't you eating? Is something troubling you, girly?" the duchess questioned after a while, having noticed Fiona pushing the food around her plate.

Fiona hesitated only a moment before speaking. "Actually, yes. The fortnight the Duke had given me to prove myself will end in three days. So what do you plan to do, your grace? Will I keep my position here or will I be asked to leave?"

"You're forthright," the duchess snorted.

"Well?" Fiona prodded impatiently.

"You'd be a fool if you hadn't figured it out until now. And I doubt you're a fool," she smiled.

"So I'm hoping that you want me to stay?" Fiona raised a brow.

"I do."

Fiona let out a breath she hadn't known she'd been holding.

"Thank you, your grace. You don't know how much I need this position."

"I can guess. But I suspect I need you more."

"What do you mean?"

"Oh it's nothing."

"Oh no, you don't. What is it?"

"So you think you can be impertinent just because your position here is secure now?" the duchess huffed.

"But I was impertinent even before that, wasn't I?" Fiona countered with a smile.

"Yes," the duchess chuckled. "Very well, though I doubt you'd understand."

"Try me."

"You see, Nate and I don't share a very good relationship. So having you around is a great comfort."

"What? But I always see him asking after you and—"

"He does care about me. And he is good son. But we hardly have any sort of relationship anymore. Why do you think he wanted to hire a companion so desperately? He knew I needed someone. And he isn't willing to be there for me. He isn't willing to let me be there for him either."

Fiona looked on in confusion. She'd never guessed that such turmoil existed between the mother and son.

"Have you tried talking to him about this?"

"You want me to tell him that I'm lonely and want him to spend more time with me? That I miss him?" the Duchess looked positively appalled at the prospect of admitting her weakness.

"Well, yes. How else is he supposed to know?"

She'd never understand these people of rank, Fiona thought. She'd never faced such problems with her parents when they'd lived or even her nana.

"Oh he knows. I've seen the guilt on his face every time he leaves on his unnecessary jaunts to London."

"He didn't go to London once ever since I've come."

"That's because he feels duty bound to stay—with me being unwell and all. Also, it's his engagement ball in a few days. It will follow the week long house party."

Fiona digested that bit of information, disturbed by the churning in her belly.

Then she looked at the duchess's forlorn face and immediately chastised herself for being so selfish.

She'd been wrong about the woman. A companion was not what she needed, it was her son that she wanted. But she was too bloody stubborn—like her son—to admit it. And Fiona would be damned if she didn't at least try to fix what had been broken.

Chapter 10

Fiona tiptoed about the silent hallway of the Duke's family wing, holding the candelabra before her to illuminate her path.

"This has to be the most harebrained idea to have ever struck you, Fiona Butterworth," she whispered to herself. "Oh wonderful, now I'm talking to myself."

She let out a little "eep" when her hip banged against a large porcelain vase. It tilted this was and that before it teetered over to the left.

"Oh no you don't," Fiona gasped and practically threw herself down to keep it from falling.

She let out a sigh of relief when it landed solidly on her hand. She would throw herself into the cold waters of the Thames before she let herself be responsible for the destruction of another article in the Duke's household. She had three vases and one sculpture on her conscience as such. Who needed so many vases anyway?

She tried to get up, but in her haste one of the candles had broken and her sudden movement caused it to fall on her hand—flame and all.

"Goddamnit," she cursed loudly and then shook off her hand. This had to be bad omen of some sort—almost breaking a precious vase and burning one's hand in one night usually was.

But it was too late for second thoughts, she thought to herself as she set the vase straight and got up. Fiona dusted her clothes with her free hand, ignoring the burning in her right hand.

"In for a penny, in for a pound," she huffed and resumed making her way towards the Duke's chambers.

And then she was standing outside the grand door. She wiped her sweaty palms on her skirts and raised her hand to knock.

Was this wise?

Of course it wasn't, she thought with a snort.

But she had to do it. For the duchess.

It was the least she could do after the woman had been so kind to her and make her position a permanent one.

She knocked thrice before she could change her mind.

In about five seconds, the door swung open—to reveal the Duke himself(who else was she expecting?), the usual scowl in place.

Nate was silent as he looked at the woman standing outside his door.

Surely he had to be dreaming? Surely the woman had to have some sense to not knock at an unmarried gentleman's door at this ungodly hour—with her hair unbound?

"Your grace?" came her very real voice. Of course he was not so lucky for this to have been a mere dream.

He looked behind her to make sure no one had seen her and pulled her inside before shutting the door behind her.

"Have you lost your mind?" he barked, not bothering to sound civilised. She didn't deserve it—this mad woman.

"I know what this looks like, but I am only here to talk," she said stoutly, even as a blush stained her cheeks and her eyes hesitantly scanned his torso.

His unclothed torso. Bloody hell.

"And you couldn't wait until—I don't know, say a more decent hour of the day?" he snapped, tugging on his shirt.

"Of course I considered the possibility. But you see, I heard from the servants that you would be leaving to town by dawn tomorrow. And I didn't know when you'd return. After you return, you will be busy with the preparations for your house party and then the house party will begin and you know how those last forever. Also—"

"Enough," he roared.

"—this is matter of utmost importance and hence cannot wait," she finished anyway, although she did look uncertain now.

Good.

Nate gulped in two long breaths. He wasn't being a bear unreasonably. He had reasons—three very reasonable reasons. One, there was a very delectable female in his bed chamber in the middle of the night. Two, he was attracted to said female—there was no denying that anymore. And three, just the sight of her with her hair flowing down to her waist and her trembling mouth made him want to throw her onto his bed and have his wicked way with her. Especially after he'd spent the better part of the day fantasising about that very mouth.

She causally moved towards the fireplace, which was on the opposite side of door—obviously to make sure he didn't throw her out.

But faced with the options of throwing her out or kissing her senseless, the former seemed the wisest.

"I will speak to you after my return and not before that, Miss Butterworth. So get out of my chamber," he growled.

She flinched but straightened.

"I apologise for inconveniencing you, your grace. But this conversation will take place now," she said haughtily.

Did she not have the fear of god in her?

Nate lunged at her and caught her hand, ready to bodily drag her out but her yelp caught him. It wasn't one of surprise, it was one of pain. He wasn't even holding her in a painful grip...

He swung around and released her hand. Her lips were pursed as if she were in pain and here eyes were squeezed shut. She clutched the hand he'd just seized in her own as it trembled and swore.

"What's wrong?" he asked gruffly.

"It's nothing, your grace. Now if you would just listen to me, you'd—"

"What happened to your hand?" he strode up to her and tenderly lifted the hand she'd been nursing. He turned her towards the fire so he could see more clearly.

There was a red patch of about one inch diameter on the back of her palm.

"You burnt yourself?" he asked as he made her sit on a chair.

"Just now," she nodded hesitantly.

"How?" he asked as he moved towards the bed stand where a jug of clean water rested. He picked it up and poured the contents into a bowl before bringing it to her.

"I accidentally dropped a candle on it. I think it was the hot wax more than the flame," she mumbled as he carefully dipped her hand into the bowl.

"You ought to be more careful," he chastised her, not liking the pinched look on her face.

"Are you sure your father was a vicar?" he asked to take her mind off her pain.

"Yes, why do you ask?"

"Well, from the way you swear, I thought he might've been a sailor."

"I have my Nana to thank for that," she snorted.

Nate wanted to ask more but he refrained.

He got up again and brought an ointment this time. He held her palm in his and carefully applied it on her wound. "I don't have any bandages here, I'm afraid."

Her only response was her shallow breathing. Nate looked up to see that it was not pain that caused it—but something else. Something that quickened his pulse.

He was about to lean in but then caught himself. This wouldn't do.

He got up from where he'd been kneeling on the floor and took a seat opposite her.

"Now about that important conversation of yours..."

****

Hello dear readers, I wish all of you a very happy Diwali! And to those of you who don't know, Diwali is the Indian festival is lights and it's kind of a big deal here. Hope y'all enjoy the chapter. Much love Ashmita

Chapter 11

"You were wrong about your mother," Fiona said, fervently praying she wasn't messing this up.

"Wrong how?" he arched his brow, arrogant as ever.

"She does not need a companion, your grace."

"You do realise that you're jeopardising your position, don't you?" he asked, a hint of amusement in his voice.

"I do," she sighed.

"If she doesn't need you, then what does she need, Miss Butterworth?" he asked, solemn once again.

"You."

"What do you mean? I am her son and I live with her," he scoffed.

"Not all the time. When was the last time you had a proper conversation with her?"

That seemed to make him angry for he stood up, his frown sliding back into place.

"You are in no position to question my relationship with my mother, you hear me?" he all but growled.

"And yet here I am, questioning it," she replied, refusing to let him cow her.

He strode up to her and placed his hands on either sides of her chair, his face only inches away from hers, effectively trapping her.

"I take very good care of my mother. I make sure she never has to ask for anything. And speaking of not always being here in the country—I have work to do outside of this estate. I must attend the parliament and I have friends in London. I hired you precisely for this reason—so you could entertain her during my absence. If you cannot do it then feel free to leave."

"Now look here, Duke," Fiona began, feeling the anger rising in her. "I am perfectly able to do my duty. But that isn't what your mother needs. Surely you don't need to go to London so often? And even when you are here, you barely spare any time for her. You're locked up in your god forsaken study doing God knows what when you can spend some of that time in your mother's company!" she finished with a lift of her chin. That brought her face closer to his but she was past caring.

"I am not discussing this with you," he said, his voice dangerously low.

"Why not?" she shot back.

"Because it is none of your bloody business," he shouted.

Fiona flinched, but she wasn't going to back down now.

"Anything that concerns her grace, concerns me. I'm her paid companion after all. And this is a part of my job," she said and stared into his eyes.

But he was looking down—at her mouth. Fiona felt her traitorous heart give a fierce kick in her chest.

"Say something," she huffed, annoyed of the effect he had on her. His blue eyes that had turned dark shot to hers. And then he pulled her up and kissed her.

Somewhere at the back of her mind, she knew that this wasn't supposed to happen. She knew that she wasn't supposed to allow his hands to roam her back so freely or allow him to plaster her body to his. She certainly knew that she shouldn't have lifted her hands and twined them about his neck.

But she was far beyond caring and she suspected he was too.

He wasn't kissing her softly, the way he had that morning. He was kissing her angrily—as if punishing her for talking too much. But she was angry too. And she parried back, meeting his sensual assault with one of her own.

"What are you doing to me?" he murmured.

"I suspect the same thing that you are doing to me," she replied shakily.

He kissed her again, although he was more gentle this time, slowly coaxing her lips apart.

Fiona let our out a sigh of longing.

This was beyond her wildest dreams. That the Duke was the one kissing her so made it all the more special.

She could feel the heat of him, only her gown and his linen shirt separating their bodies. His hand that had been stroking her back slowly slid forward. He skimmed her waist before resting it on her bosom.

For a second, she stood frozen. The intimacy of the caress stopping all thoughts in her mind.

But only for a second.

Then she pushed him away, positive her cheeks were red as tomatoes.

"You are betrothed, your grace," she said gently.

"You didn't seem to remember that a few second ago," he said, his breathing still laboured.

Fiona stared at him. "I was not the one who initiated this."

"Oh really? If I remember correctly, you came to my chamber in a state of undress. You insisted on staying in spite of my telling you to leave," he said, his anger returning.

"I only wanted to talk!"

"Yes, I suppose we've spoken enough. You may leave now."

Fiona gave him a curt nod and began walking towards the door. Just as her hand landed on the latch, he spoke.

"Fiona, wait."

She paused but she didn't turn around. Her pride was in tatters and she was holding in her tears with a lot of difficulty.

"I sorry," he groaned. "I didn't mean any of that. I take responsibility for whatever happened. I lost control."

Fiona turned around slowly, hoping the dark would hide her expression from him.

"As you so kindly pointed out, I didn't object either. So I think it's better if we stay away from each other."

She held her breath, waiting for him to refuse. Hoping, silly girl that was, that he would tell her that he couldn't stay away from her.

"Yes, you're right."

Fiona nodded stiffly and slipped out before he could say something more. He'd done enough damage for one evening as such.

****

After Fiona left, Nate poured himself a glass of whiskey. Strange how he'd started drinking more than he usually did ever since she'd come into his life.

Oh but he'd been an utter arse now.

She'd come with pure intentions—risking her reputation for his mother and he'd repaid her like this. By mauling her and kissing her.

His mother. Yes, that was what had made him so angry. Hearing from Fiona what he already knew, hearing her berate him for it reminded him of his weakness. Of how badly he'd bungled his relationship with his mother.

But he was too proud to simply apologise to her for not being there for her.

Then again, he was making it up to her, wasn't he? He was getting married and soon she'd have grandchildren to coddle.

Married.

Sophia.

How could he have forgotten about her? Yes, he wasn't in love with her and he had chosen her for more practical reasons, but he respected her. He'd certainly intended to be a loyal husband.

And how could he go behind her back in such a fashion?

The worst part was, the thought of sharing a bed with Sophia left a bad taste in his mouth.

She wouldn't respond to his kisses the way Fiona had. She wouldn't argue with him so fearlessly for a cause that had nothing to do with her.

Nate scrubbed his hand against his face.

Goodness gracious, what had he gotten himself into?!

There was only one thing to do now—stay away from Fiona as she'd herself suggested.

Chapter 12

The next week went by in a daze. Fiona and the Duke had avoided each other all the while. Only on one occasion had they come face to face—after he'd returned from town. They'd greeted each other stiffly and then had dashed off into their respective havens.

The entire household could sense that their lively and talkative Miss Butterworth was now solemn and quiet. But they were happy that she was here to stay—now that the duchess had made her position permanent.

As for Fiona herself, she'd decided to forgive the Duke and herself for that night. She'd blamed the lateness of the hour to justify her actions but she knew better. Then again, it was pointless to berate herself. What was done was done. She'd just make sure that it never happened again.

After that she was too busy to indulge in self pity because the house party was to begin. The Duchess—who was now on her feet again was overlooking the preparations and asked for Fiona's opinion on everything. What was ironical was that Fiona didn't know a thing about house parties and balls. She had received an extensive education from her father, but her knowledge was limited to history, mathematics, greek and basic sciences.

She could run her tiny home well enough, of course. But that didn't mean she could take over the management of a Duke's household with ease.

While she found it odd that the dowager duchess was taking her help, she didn't protest. At this point, she would welcome anything challenging just to keep her mind off the handsome Duke that resided there.

****

Nate stood by his fiancé, brooding all the while as he took in Fiona's appearance as she flitted about but never left his mother's side for too long.

She shouldn't have been here. But his mother had sputtered some nonsense about there not being enough women to match the number of men. He knew this was all a ploy because his mother wanted to catch a husband for her dear companion. Not that he cared, he told himself.

He'd agreed to his mother's plea, thinking there'd be no harm.

But he hadn't imagined that Fiona would be dressed in the soft, practical yet pretty muslin gown that she was wearing now. The neckline was much lower than that of her usual dark gowns. And that displayed quite a lot of her creamy chest and swanlike neck. He didn't mind the view. But he hated that the other men were noticing her untouched beauty and were just as taken by her as him.

God damnit, but this was a disaster.

He'd made an enormous mistake by agreeing to his mother's request. He'd been an idiot to think that it was perfectly alright to have the woman he was going to marry and the woman he was lusting after under the same roof. He was a cad, an utter ass.

Sophia touched his arm and Nate turned towards her, half hoping she hadn't caught him staring at his mother's companion and hoping more secretly that she had.

"Are you alright?" she smiled at him.

Nate nodded stiffly, oddly untouched by her smile.

"Who is that woman?"

"Who?" Nate feigned nonchalance.

"That plain woman in the pink gown, next to your mother," Sophia said, her eyes twinkling.

Nate was about to tell her that Fiona was not plain, but he held himself back. He looked at Sophia carefully and found that there was no malice on her face. She looked like she'd just made an innocent observation.

"You mean Miss Butterworth? She is mother's new companion," he said.

"Isn't she a little too young to be a competent companion?"

"I wouldn't question Fiona on her competency were I you," he chuckled. He realised what he'd just said a little too late.

This time Sophia was looking at him more carefully, her green eyes searching his face keenly.

"It appears you know her quite well," she said finally.

"I couldn't allow just anyone near my mother," he shrugged noncommittally while mentally chiding himself.

If Fiona was to continue working for him, it wouldn't do if Sophia developed any form of jealousy towards her.

Sophia nodded, apparently satisfied with his answer.

But Nate knew he couldn't afford to repeat such a mistake.

"Why don't you introduce us? It would be prudent if she continues working here after we marry," she smiled shyly.

Again, Nate was unaffected but he murmured his assent and began leading her towards where Fiona stood, surrounded by some people.

Fiona's carefree laughter reached him before he could reach her. His muscles tightened reflexively and he had to force himself to relax, to appear composed.

"I hope Nathaniel and I aren't interrupting," Sophia said breezily as they joined the group. Everyone was loud in their reassurances that they were very pleased to have her join their conversation.

Only Fiona was silent. At first her eyes had widened on seeing him. Then her gaze slid to Sophia on his arm. Her animation as she was recounting some antidote immediately vanished.

After that, she refused to look at him.

"Miss Butterworth," he started, leaving her no choice but to acknowledge him. "This is Lady Sophia. And this is Miss Butterworth, Sophia."

Fiona curtseyed and greeted her with a smile.

"I'm pleased to make your acquaintance, Miss Butterworth," Sophia smiled back. "I hope we shall get on well. I understand you will remain here until some gentleman sweeps you off your feet. And while I'm sure her grace loves having you around, I wouldn't wish a sweet girl like you to rusticate here in the country."

Nate frowned. Is that what Sophia thought about the country? Did she or did she not know that they would be spending the majority of the year here?

"I'm sure we will get on very well," Fiona said politely, ignoring the rest of Sophia's musings. But the other gentlemen weren't so eager to let her words pass.

"Of course! With you off the market, I'd despaired that I'd not find any woman worth her salt, Lady Sophia. But meeting Miss Butterworth has indeed relieved me in that regard," Lord Winston grinned down at Fiona. The other men murmured their agreements.

And although Fiona blushed, it was more out of embarrassment. But that didn't mean that Nate didn't wasn't to strangle Winston.

"You are much too kind, Lord Winston," Fiona replied.

"Lord Winston is rarely kind. I believe he is taken by you, Miss Butterworth," Sophia tittered.

Fiona began to stutter under all of their watchful gazes and Nate wanted to strangle his fiancé for making her uncomfortable. Unlike Sophia, Fiona wasn't used to the attentions of men, hell this was probably the first house party she was attending.

"Miss Butterworth, I think my mother is looking for you," Nate interrupted them. Fiona shot him a grateful glance before murmuring her apologies to them and dashing off. And in a few minutes, Sophia was called by one of her friends and she too, left.

"It's just unfair that you've kept her hidden all this while, your grace" Winston whined, just as Sophia left.

"Yes, isn't it enough that you have Lady Sophia?" Baron Grayson muttered.

Winston was handsome and a few years his junior. Since he was an Earl, it would be quite shocking if he set his sights on Fiona. But such unions weren't uncommon. And that made Nate angry. He couldn't let that ass have Fiona, she deserved better.

"I'd advice you to stay away from Miss Butterworth."

"Why?" Winston watched him shrewdly.

"Because she is in my employment and I am responsible for her."

"She isn't a child, Duke. I'm sure she can take care of herself. And my intentions are pure, I assure you. Surely you cannot begrudge me then?"

"Is it marriage you're offering then?" Nate challenged, the reckless words falling from his mouth before he could stop himself.

"If she'd have me," Winston grinned. He'd never been able to resist a challenge and Nate had been a fool to issue one.

"I propose a wager that Winston here will woo Miss Butterworth by the end of this house party," the idiot Baron spoke up.

Before Nate knew it, there were several men wagering on Winston.

And he knew that in his fit of jealously, he'd probably made the biggest mistake of his life.

****

Hey guys, I'm sorry I'm a little late but I hope all of you had a great thanksgiving. Love, Ashmita

Chapter 13

The next morning, a number of the ladies and gentlemen were seen riding about the country side. The weather was fine and the day bright.

Fiona was lurking outside, unsure of what to do. The duchess had ordered her out and commanded that she enjoy herself. Whatever did that mean?

From the corner of her eye, she spotted the Duke and Lady Sophia, riding side by side. They did indeed make a fine sight, the pair of them. The Lady was a beautiful woman and when Fiona had seen her yesterday for the first time, she'd felt like a tiny, inconsequential bug—not worthy of breathing the same air as her. In daylight, she was even more dazzling. Her green riding attire was immaculate, showcasing her perfect figure and her glorious hair cascaded down her back in soft waves. Not to mention, the two of them together looked like they'd jumped straight out of a painting. And in their presence, Fiona couldn't help but feel small.

She cringed at the direction of her thoughts.

You are just as worthy as them, she told herself sternly. And if someone could make her feel small, it was herself.

"Miss Butterworth!" someone bellowed. Fiona groaned before turning to see who it was.

Lord Winston.

"Good morning, my lord. How can I help you this morn?" she fixed a smile upon her lips.

"By slowing down?" he replied as he jogged to her side. "I've been calling out your name."

Fiona chuckled. "I'm afraid I didn't hear you."

"Is there something you need?" Fiona questioned once he'd reached her side.

"Good God, woman! Has no one ever approached you to simply for the pleasure of your company?"

"No," she said with a small shrug.

"Well, there's always a first time," he huffed, looking affronted on her behalf.

Fiona couldn't help but smile. Her smile more genuine this time. Yes, Lord Winston unnerved her a little—almost every guest here did. But he wasn't so bad. Maybe she could do without all the attention he was showering on her, but she didn't mind his company. He seemed amiable enough—not bothered by her lack of a rank.

"Shall we ride?" he asked politely.

"I can't ride. I never had the chance to learn."

"Very well. Shall I walk with you then?"

"Yes," Fiona replied. Lord Winston smiled and took the hand lying limply by her side and put it on his arm.

He was quite talkative but also knowledgable. He asked for her opinion on various matters and Fiona found herself enjoying their light but witty banter.

More than once, Fiona had noticed the Duke staring at them from a distance. He had looked angry and his face looked like it was set in stone. Fiona decided that it was best if she ignored him.

"I like you, Miss Butterworth," Lord Winston smiled down at her.

"A lot of people do, Lord Winston," Fiona grinned cheekily at him.

He threw his head back and laughed, the sound loud and jolly. It also drew the attention of many people, including that of the Duke and Fiona was just a little embarrassed at all the attention directed towards her.

"Call me Robert, please. And give me the permission to call you by your given name," he said, his eyes intent, all traces of amusement gone.

Fiona wondered if it was proper. But he was an Earl and surely she wasn't so prudish as to deny him this. And she knew that he had only friendship in mind.

"Alright, Robert," she smiled and the Earl smiled back at her.

****

Nate was seething as he tried to find his mother's companion. He'd scoured the entire house and there was no trace of her. Now he was on the balcony, hoping his mother would know where she was.

Trouble.

That's what she was. She wasn't just troublesome. She was trouble personified.

"Mother, where's Miss Butterworth?" Nate barked.

"She's gone to fetch me my shawl," his mother replied, her brows raised at his tone.

"Send her to my study the minute she gets here."

With that he turned and left, not even waiting for his mother's response. Then he went down to his study and waited.

After half an hour, a knock sounded.

"Enter," he said, trying his best to control his temper. Fiona entered, her eyes wide with confusion.

"What took you so long?"

"Forgive me if I'm unable to be present at your ever beck and call. I have to attend to your mother, you see," she snapped, shutting the door behind her.

"Now what did you wish to speak of?" she asked, looking impatient. As if she had somewhere to be. Or someone to see...

Nate felt his anger return with a vengeance.

"You shall cease talking to Winston," he barked.

If he'd expected her to heed his words and assure him that she would do so immediately, he'd been sorely mistaken.

"Why?" she shot back.

"Because I am your employer and I demand it from you!" he bellowed.

She flinched at his volume but stood ramrod straight, her hands folded in front of her. Nate tried to ignore how they pushed her bosom upwards—the swells rising above her bodice but in vain.

"And I demand a reasonable explanation."

He was riveted by her. She was angry, her eyes shooting daggers at him and her stance resembling that of a woman poised to attack.

And all he could think of was how she'd react if he pressed his lips to hers. Would she kiss him back, refusing to back down as she had that night in his chamber or would she scratch his eye balls out?

Something told him the latter was the most probable outcome.

And so he remained where he was, finding that he wasn't angry anymore—just incredibly annoyed. And a little uncomfortable. What was he to say to her?

"His intentions aren't right," he said finally.

Fiona merely raised her brow, signalling for him to continue.

"He aims at taking advantage of you, Fiona. Winston is a charming man and I'm sure you find yourself drawn towards him. But this will lead to nothing. He only wishes to dally with you."

"Then he's not very different from you, I see," she replied coldly.

Nate stiffened.

"You worry needlessly, your grace. I'm a big girl and I can take care of myself. Also, I find I am immune to the Earl's charms, abundant as they are," she added before he could say anything.

"As relieved as I am to hear it, I would like to warn you again. The men are already wagering on him, he's confident that you will accept his proposal of marriage before this house party ends."

Fiona began to laugh. At first Nate was annoyed, but then he found himself being drawn to her laughter—to her.

"What is so amusing?" he asked huskily, coming to a halt only one feet away from her.

"That the Earl would consider marriage to me," she laughed again. "Surely you jest."

"I don't."

She stopped laughing immediately at his serious tone, although her lips were still stretched into a wide smile.

Before he could stop himself, he bent forward and caught her lips with his. The air around the fairly crackled and Nate had to fight for breath, the feel of her too intoxicating.

But it was over in a few moments because Fiona pushed him back, her eyes accusing.

"I think you've been advising me to stay away from the wrong man," she whispered.

And then she turned, threw open the door and fled.

Leaving Nate there feeling strangely bereft and like a thousand kinds of ass.

Chapter 14

"You're not considering accepting Lord Winston's proposal, are you?" the dowager Duchess asked Fiona as she flitted about the chamber, arranging everything the duchess would need by her bedside.

"Well, considering how he hasn't issued any proposal as yet, the point is moot, don't you think?" Fiona shot back.

"Yes, but what if he does? Will you accept?" the Duchess insisted, a frown creasing her brow.

Fiona sighed and sat on the foot of the bed.

"The truth is, I do not know."

"Does that mean you have feelings for him?"

"Not that I know of," Fiona chuckled.

"Then you have no reason to accept his proposal."

"But there is. I can't remain her me forever. I need to marry."

I need to get away from this house, from the Duke who holds my heart in his fist.

"You've never mentioned your desire to marry before. And I thought you didn't want to leave me or your Nana," the Duchess retorted, her voice taking on an edge.

"I don't. I'll take Nana with me wherever I go and you'll have Lady Sophia to keep you company."

The Duchess huffed.

"I heard something about a wager. If that pup is wagering on you, then he can't be very serious about you, can he?"

Like mother, like son, Fiona thought.

"I asked the Earl about that," Fiona nodded. "He said that his friends came up with that and he agreed to it just to annoy the Duke."

"Nathaniel was annoyed, was he?" she asked, her eyes lighting up.

Fiona shrugged noncommittally.

"I still think this discussion unwarranted. After all, I doubt the Earl is going to propose to a lowly companion like me. We have a healthy friendship and I dearly hope that it remains that way."

"There's nothing lowly about you," the Duchess admonished.

"Be that as it may, he isn't going to fall for me overnight," Fiona chuckled.

The Duchess huffed again.

"Take yourself to bed. Tomorrow is going to be busy. A few more guests are arriving on the morrow."

Fiona nodded and bid her a good night.

When she entered the chamber assigned to her, her knees gave way and she landed on her bottom on the floor.

She buried her face against her knees and let lose all the tears that she'd been holding the entire day.

Oh but it hurt.

It hurt to see the Duke dancing attendance on his fiancé. It hurt even more when she thought of his kiss and how he'd tried to talk to her after that.

This was another reason she wanted to be gone from here.

She strongly doubted the Earl would propose—his behaviour had given no such indication. And she'd surely not encourage him to issue one. But still, if he did offer for her despite all the odds, Fiona wouldn't dismiss it immediately. There was much to think about.

Marrying him would be the perfect escape. She did enjoy his company and maybe she'd even come to love him as much as she loved the Duke. Then again, in her heart, she knew she'd never be able to live with another man.

That brought on a fresh batch of tears.

It was funny how much she'd begun to cry ever since she'd fallen for the Duke. She hadn't even broken down as she did now when Nana and her didn't even have enough food to sate their hunger.

She huffed and pushed herself off the floor. After putting on her night gown she dragged herself to the bed. She was extremely tired and was hoping that she'd fall asleep immediately but no such thing happened.

She lay awake while her brain tortured her with images of the Duke and Lady Sophia together.

At one point, she imagined the Duke kissing his fiancé the way he'd kissed her and that was more than she could endure.

She squeezed her eyes shut and rubbed her hands against them as if to erase the disturbing image.

By the time she fell asleep, it was nearly dawn.

Fiona woke up, bleary eyed and morose.

When she got down, she spotted a number of people who weren't present yesterday.

She smiled at some of them as she made her way toward the breakfast parlour.

Much to her annoyance, Lady Sophia and the Duke were present as well. Just what she needed.

"Good morning, my lady," Fiona said when Lady Sophia noticed her presence.

"Good morning," she returned, her gaze travelling down Fiona's simple yellow muslin gown. "Are you always up this late in the morning?" she murmured and looked at the Duke as if wanting him to say something. But the Duke said nothing and only looked at her through hooded eyes.

"No, today's an exception," Fiona smiled lightly and piled her plate with some eggs. After last night's weeping episode, she was ravenous this morning and the last thing she wanted was to have a discussion on all of her flaws with Lady Sophia.

"Then I assume Lord Winston's thoughts kept you awake most of the night," she tittered. Fiona was beginning to hate that sound.

"Sophia—" the Duke began to reprimand her but the Lady was having none of it.

"I only jest, Nathaniel. And Miss Butterworth is aware of that, aren't you?" she looked to Fiona, her eyes wide.

Fiona nodded jerkily.

"And I must ask you, Miss Butterworth, where have you purchased this gown from?"

Before Fiona could open her mouth, she continued. "I don't ask for myself, of course. I can never be seen wearing something as plain as this. I ask for my lady's maid—she is of your ilk, you see."

That was definitely meant to be an insult if Fiona had ever heard one.

A hushed silence descended over the parlour, everyone surprised by Lady Sophia's behaviour.

Again the Duke opened his mouth to reprimand her but Fiona beat him to it. It wouldn't do if he scolded his fiancé on her behalf.

"What is your lady's maid's name, my lady? If you could be so good as to tell me, I'll find her myself and tell her," Fiona smiled politely.

Lady Sophia opened and closed her mouth like a fish.

"Please excuse me," Fiona said and got up from the table. Honestly, she'd lost her appetite. "The Duchess must be looking for me."

And then she did something she'd never done.

She fled.

Chapter 15

"Sophia, we need to talk," Nate said to his fiancé in a voice that brooked no argument. The other people looked wary.

Yes, what Sophia has done was despicable and Nate's control was hanging by a thread, but still. She was going to be his wife and to them, Fiona was nobody. She didn't have a rank to back her and she was his mother's companion.

But he'd be damned if he let this go. Maybe Fiona didn't matter to them, but she sure as hell mattered to him. He knew that much now.

Sophia looked a little uncertain but flashed everyone a bright smile and stood up. She latched on to his arm as he walked out of the parlour.

"Where are we going, Nathaniel?" she asked nervously.

"Somewhere private."

"Are you finally going to kiss me?" she asked breathlessly.

Nate stopped walking and she nearly collided with him.

"We are going to talk about your behaviour with Fiona."

"Oh so now you're on first name basis," she said bitterly. "Are you honestly going to take her side? And I didn't even say anything offensive!"

"I chose you because you seemed like you had a sound mind. I thought you had polish. Clearly I was wrong," Nate said coldly.

"You're saying all this to me for her?! For that lowly, cheap nothing?" she shrieked.

"You will speak of her with nothing but respect," Nate growled. "She has done nothing to deserve your ire."

"Hasn't she? Every time I look at my fiancé, I find him looking at her. You didn't even look happy to see me."

Nate sighed. His head had began to throb. What was he to say to Sophia? That he wanted his mother's companion? That she affected him the way no other woman had?

"I was happy to see you. And I'm keeping an eye on her. She is an easy target for all the gentlemen and since she's under my protection, I must make sure nobody tries to take advantage of her."

At least that was part of the truth.

His attraction to Fiona would wear off, he told himself. It was more important that he repair the damage on his relationship with Sophia. She was going to be his wife. Sophia was good for the dukedom, for the name of his family. Fiona wasn't.

Sophia didn't look like she believed him but her grip on his arm loosened.

"I shall endeavour to be more polite henceforth."

"Thank you."

Nate knew where he stood in her eyes. She didn't want love. She wanted to be a duchess. Which was just as well—he didn't need love either.

****

Nate was trying to find Fiona. Again.

The woman sure knew how to disappear. He'd looked everywhere. And even his mother didn't know where she was.

He knew she hadn't eaten, so he'd packed some scones in a little napkin. He hoped it would make up for what Sophia had said to her.

Nate knew he shouldn't be chasing after her this way. And he'd tried to convince himself that it didn't matter if her feelings got a little hurt.

But he hadn't been able to. He had to make things right with her. Fiona was one of the few people he was most comfortable with and he didn't want to ruin that. He also owed her an apology for yesterday's kiss.

He stopped a nearby footman and asked him about Fiona.

"I saw her heading into the maze, your grace," he replied. Nate thanked him and took off on a run heading to the maze.

He quickly made his way towards the centre, his heart racing—he didn't know why.

As he neared the centre though, he heard laughter.

What?

And then he saw her. Fiona sitting on a small blanket by the fountain.

But she wasn't alone.

Sitting opposite to her was Winston. Food spread out between them. And both of them were smiling, their profiles to him.

A fury unlike any he'd ever experienced seized Nate. His head felt close to exploding and his fists clenched on his sides.

And it wasn't just anger he felt. There was a healthy dose of hurt. He felt betrayed. Which was bloody ridiculous. He knew it and yet that didn't stop him from growling her name.

She turned toward him, a startled expression on his face. Winston merely looked put out.

"What is it, your grace? Is it your mother?" she got up and walked towards him hurriedly, her yellow skirts tangling with her legs, a frown creasing her brow.

"No," he said shortly.

"Then?"

"What are you doing with him? All alone?" he hated how wounded he sounded.

"Not that I owe you any explanation, but this wasn't a planned rendezvous. I was here—sulking. And Lord Winston must have heard about what happened because he asked for a picnic basket and set out to find me," she replied.

"I brought you scones," he said, sounding every inch a petulant child as he dragged out the napkin from his coat.

"Thank you," she murmured, her expression unreadable as S he took it from him. "I'm too full to eat anything just now, I shall eat them later."

"Is there a problem?" Winston called from behind them.

"Yes," Nate growled at the same time Fiona said, "no."

"Well, what is it?" he asked again.

"It's nothing, my lord. I'll be there in a moment," she replied, her eyes pleaded with Nate all the while to keep quiet.

"Why are you here, your grace?" she asked him softly.

"I knew you must be hungry," he huffed.

"Then can I go back?"

"No. I also wanted to apologise on Sophia's behalf."

"That isn't necessary. I'm sure the Lady didn't mean any offence. Besides, she didn't say anything untrue," she whispered.

"It was utter rubbish, you hear me," he said fiercely and clutched her hand in his, his eyes burning into hers. "A mere rank cannot decide your worth. You're far above her. Far above everyone else here."

"Why did you choose to marry Lady Sophia, your grace? Did you fall in love with her?"

Nate was flustered by her question. "I—" he started but began to stutter.

"I thought so," she smiled warily.

"Fiona—"

"Let go of my hand, your grace. Please."

Nate released her hand. He began to follow her but she turned around and stared at him.

"You can't ask me to leave. This is my house. I own this place."

Fiona shrugged, but Nate had never felt so small.

He swore and left the maze, eager to get away from that damned woman who'd managed to get under his skin.

Chapter 16

The next afternoon, Fiona was seated with Lord Winston—he rarely left her alone. Most of the time, she didn't mind...even the duchess's disgruntlement over his attentions only amused her. But today was not one of those days.

Ever since he'd left her in the maze yesterday, the Duke had been different. She didn't catch him staring at her at inopportune times. He didn't try to seek her out with one excuse or another. He didn't stare at Lord Winston when he tried to monopolise on her time.

If anything, he was directing all of his attention on his fiancé—as it should've been. He'd whisper in her ear and spend as much time with her as possible. Lady Sophia was looking at her smugly but she wasn't torturing Fiona with any snide remarks.

She should be relieved, she knew. To have the Duke ignore her was what she'd wanted from the start. He was treating her as if she was no more than his mother's companion—and she was. Fiona knew her place. But that didn't mean her heart didn't ache.

It was physical—the pain. Her throat felt like it was clogged and she just wanted to scream and cry just to release the hurt.

She was surprised by the force of her reaction. She'd never been too sorrowful or emotional. Even when the times were hard, she would find a way to laugh it off.

Being desolate wasn't something she was familiar with.

"You seem upset, Fiona. Is everything alright?" Lord Winston asked, a concerned expression on his face.

Fiona nodded tightly, but her eyes didn't move from the sight before her.

Lord Winston followed the line of her vision and immediately understood. It was the Duke. He was feeding some pastry to Lady Sophia who took little bites.

"Fiona..." he began but she held up her hand. He knew. He knew and he wasn't angry. He sounded sympathetic. But Fiona didn't want sympathy.

"I'm fine. You worry needlessly. I just need some fresh air," she said and shot him an apologetic glance and stood.

"Would you like me to come along with you?"

"No, I wish to be alone."

She didn't wait to hear his response.

She exited the hall and wandered outside. Where was she to go?

Her feet automatically began carrying her towards the stables.

Although she couldn't ride, Fiona had discovered that she enjoyed being in the company of horses. They soothed her. After the house party had begun, Fiona would often visit the stables.

She hoped it would be empty at this time.

Fiona immediately went to her favourite filly's stall.

"Hello, Cindy," she smiled and the horse neighed happily. She began to lip at Fiona's hair as soon as she was close enough.

"I didn't bring you any apples today, I'm afraid," she grinned.

The horse let out what seemed like a sigh but seemed content to allow Fiona to brush her.

After a while of confessing her feelings to Cindy and crying, Fiona was ready to go back to the hall.

Except, she heard a voice.

"Where are you, darling? I've been looking for you."

Baron Redgrave.

Fiona retreated back into the stall.

There was only one reason the Baron would seek her out. Oh this was awful.

She'd been able to defend herself when she'd been in his employment. She used to be careful to avoid empty rooms and even when he did end up catching her alone, she'd known that help was only a a few seconds away—all she'd have to do was scream. And so even the Baron hadn't tried anything too serious—just a grope here and there.

But now...she was alone. She didn't know where the stable master was.

She had nobody who could help her and the despicable man knew it.

"I know you're in there. There's no point hiding, love. You know I'll find you. And once I find you..." he trailed off meaningfully.

Fiona frantically searched the stall for something she could use to protect herself.

Nothing.

All she had was hay.

Goodness gracious, this was a disaster.

In a few seconds, the stall door swung open and the Baron stood before her, his white teeth flashing, his eyes pure evil.

Fiona stood up.

She waited for the fear to settle in. But it never came. All she felt was anger. Anger and hatred towards this man who'd terrorised her during her youth. He didn't look quite so frightening now. And she'd be damned if she let him lay a hand on her.

She couldn't allow him to enter the stall—then she'd be trapped.

"Oh, Baron Redgrave, it was you," she sighed and took a step forward, as if relieved that it was only him.

"Were you expecting someone else?" he asked, his brow rising doubtfully.

"Well, of course." Another step. Now she was was in line with the door frame.

"Who? The Duke? I can see you've been trying to seduce him as well—I'm not the only victim to your wiles," he smiled and took a step toward her.

"Yes. I'm glad it is you and not him—but I'm sure he must be on his way at this very moment."

"Well, then I better not waste any time, huh?" he grinned and lunged at her.

"In your dreams," Fiona shouted and ducked under his arm. She knew she couldn't outrun him.

"You ungrateful bitch! You found a position here only because of me and I shall collect my fees," he shouted and ran after her.

There was a pitch fork positioned near the wall and Fiona ran towards it. She grabbed it at once and pointed it at the man.

He came to an abrupt halt.

"You wouldn't use that," he smiled.

"If you think that, then you don't know me very well."

"Put it down!"

"Not before I puncture you with it," Fiona laughed gleefully.

"Bloodthirsty, aren't you?"

She whirled around to see the Duke standing there. And although he looked to be in control, Fiona could see the rage radiating off him in waves.

"This mad woman is trying to kill me, your grace! She offered me a tumble but when I declined, she began to threaten me with this," the Baron whined, sounding every inch the distressed victim.

"He's lying," Fiona growled, aiming her makeshift weapon at him again.

"Put down the pitch fork, Fiona," he said to her even as his eyes rested on the Baron. "I don't want you to inadvertently hurt yourself," he added more softly when she began to protest.

Fiona felt the pitchfork sliding from her hand.

"He's lying, your grace."

"I swear upon my honour that she was trying to seduce me and I said no," the Baron put in, confident that he had the upper hand.

"That's funny, Redgrave. Because the last I heard, you had no honour," the Duke said softly. And when the Baron's eyes widened, the Duke took two steps forward and punched him in the face. His nose began bleeding and he crumpled to the ground.

Fiona thought he was done but he apparently wasn't because he sat atop the Baron and began punching him repeatedly.

"How dare you try and assault her? You think you could get away with something like this in my own house? You think I wouldn't find out?" he growled between punches. His entire face was covered by a mask of rage.

"You're going to end up killing him," Fiona moved towards him although she'd been tempted to do the same a few minutes ago.

She didn't want this man's death on her conscience, horrible as he was. And she didn't want the Duke to bear the burden of that either—especially not for her.

Already her heart was weakening further as she saw him defending her honour so fiercely.

She lay a hand on his shoulder and he instantly stilled.

Chapter 17

"He's unconscious," Fiona whispered to Nate. "He might die if you hit him more."

"He deserves it," Nate muttered, debating whether to heed her words.

"He does," she surprised him by saying. "But you don't deserve the consequences."

"What consequences? I'm a Duke and he's a Baron."

"Yes. And while I'm sure you might not hang, it will result in scandal and heartache for your mother. It might also affect your relationship with Lady Sophia."

"He dared to impugn your honour, he tried to rape you!"

Fiona flinched a little, the reminder of what might have happened not a pleasant one.

"I must defend your honour," he said more stubbornly.

"It's not yours to defend, your grace," she said softly, but Nate didn't miss the wistfulness in her voice. It only served to increase the pain in his chest.

"As your employer, it is," he said firmly.

"I just want him gone from here. Please..."

"Alright," he sighed heavily and got up. He dusted his clothes although they were beyond repair. The Baron mumbled something, beginning to wake up.

He opened his eyes and sneered at Fiona but his look turned fearful when Nate nudged his side with his boot.

"I want you away from my house, you hear me? If you so much as think about hurting a hair on Miss Butterworth's head even if she chooses to leave my employment in the future, I will kill you. Now get up, pack your bags and take your sorry ass out of here," Nate said menacingly.

The Baron nodded and got up to do his bidding—although he made a hideous sight...his nose was still bleeding and his face was beginning to swell.

"Wait."

He turned around, his eyes wide.

"You will apologise to her."

"There's no way in hell I'm apologising to this bitch—" he began but Nate cut him off with another punch.

"You will address her with nothing but respect," he roared.

"I'm sorry," Redgrave mumbled, nursing his newly injured jaw and ran off.

"I'm sorry you had to see that and I'm sorry he was able to get you alone this way. I never imagined he'd stoop so low," Nate murmured and walked towards where Fiona stood.

"Thank you for believing me," she smiled hesitantly.

Nate cupped her chin, his hand gentle—unlike how it had been when he'd been packing punches onto the Baron's face.

"You have no idea of how I feel about you, do you?" he asked, his voice laden with amusement.

"And let's keep it that way," she whispered.

"We should. But I can't hold myself back when it's you...I lose the control that I pride myself over. Why do you think I kissed you all those times? I have tried to resist you but—"

"Why are you telling me all this now?" she gasped, her eyes wide with hurt and something else—hope.

"So you understand when I kiss you again. And I have to do that, if only to make sure it wipes off the memory of Redgrave," he said softly and held her face in his palms as gently as he would if she were made of glass.

Fiona swallowed. She opened her mouth to say that this was wrong, that kissing would be a mistake. But no sound emerged. He was right...she needed a new memory to replace that of the Baron's. And while his kisses only reminded her of how she couldn't have him, it made her forget—if only for a few seconds.

"You don't find my kisses repulsive, do you?" He asked. Fiona almost laughed. Repulsive, indeed!

She shook her head slowly.

"Good," he murmured and then took her lips in a kiss that stole her breath.

For all his seriousness and gentlemanly veneer, her Duke was a quite talented kisser. The way his hands roamed her body bespoke of an inner restlessness.

Fiona realised he'd been scared too. She was beginning to understand him.

And he needed this kiss just as much as she did.

So she allowed her eye lids to lower and her hands to wrap about his neck. And then she gave herself up to him with a low moan.

When they pulled back, both of them were breathing hard.

"I can't get enough of you," he said hoarsely and lowered his head again.

Fiona let herself enjoy it while it lasted. He was rousing in her a tempest and she could feel it consuming her. Her toes curled in her slippers and her knees went weak.

But she didn't have to worry about falling to the ground in a heap because he was holding her tight. She was practically plastered to him!

He slowly moved her backwards until she was pressed up against a wall.

She noted more than just the movement of his mouth on hers. She felt his strong thighs pressed up against hers and her breasts tingled where they touched his chest.

Most of all, she noticed what part of his anatomy was pressed against her belly.

Goodness gracious.

Oh but she was wicked. Because it didn't repulse her or scare her—she felt powerful and curious...excited even.

"Your grace," she whispered, unsure of what to do.

"Call me Nate," he growled, his breathing harsh.

"Nate," she tested the name on her tongue. But he only growled again and began to kiss her.

"I want you so much," he said fiercely.

Pretty words, she thought to herself but refrained from responding. She didn't want to spoil this moment with conversation.

He jumped away from her when they heard a sound.

A young footman walked in, taking in the scene before him with wide eyes. It seemed unlikely that he wouldn't figure it all out.

Fiona was positive her coiffure was falling apart and that her lips were swollen. Nate looked no better—his hair was a mess (she didn't feel very guilty about it though) and his cravat was twisted.

Not to mention, they were both breathing hard.

"I'll be on my way, I just came—" he was stuttering but Nate cut him off.

"There's no need, Miss Butterworth and I were just leaving," he said calmly and offered her his arm.

She took it and they swept out of the stables as if the Duke didn't just have her against the wall a few seconds ago.

Once they were sure they were far from the footman, they burst out laughing.

"That was close," she grinned.

"Very," he chuckled, recovering slightly.

"But this can't happen again," she added more seriously. "And I'm not just saying this. I needed comfort and you comforted me, end of the story."

Nate nodded solemnly, the prospect of not being able to kiss Fiona whenever he wished (which was always) was a dull one.

But she was right. It wouldn't do if he were disloyal to his betrothed. He couldn't forget his responsibilities for a few minutes of heaven with Fiona.

And this alliance was important for his dukedom.

Or so he kept telling himself.

Chapter 18

It was a day before the house party was ending when Fiona burst into the dowager duchess's chamber.

"Lord Winston proposed to me!" she shouted as she pushed open the door.

Gaping at her from within was the Duke himself.

The duchess looked nervously between her son and her companion. And then an awkward silence ensued.

"I'm sorry, I didn't realise you were in here," Fiona stammered, cursing herself for being so repulsive.

"It's alright," he murmured. "I was bound to find out. Or were you planning on keeping it a secret all along?" he added harshly.

"Nathaniel!" his mother bellowed. "You may leave."

"I may, but I won't. Miss Butterworth is my responsibility and I will have certain answers."

The duchess tried to protest but Fiona stopped her. "It's alright, your grace. Now I will have your counsel as well as the Duke's."

"I take it you jumped with joy and said yes?" Nate growled.

"I did not. Do I look joyful to you?" Fiona gaped.

No, she looked anything but, Nate thought with some measure of relief. But that didn't mean she wouldn't say yes in the future.

If she was asking for their counsel, she was probably considering it.

Nate wanted to strangle Fiona. And that damned Winston. And his mother for looking so damned satisfied with herself.

"Well what did you tell him, my dear?" his mother asked her.

"I...um—ran off," she cringed even as she said it. His mother rolled her eyes heavenwards as if asking for divine help.

"What do I tell him?!" she asked, her face crumpling.

"You tell him no," Nate said firmly the same time his mother said, "that you'll think about it."

"She can't think about this, mother! He's not the right man for her, everyone knows that," he said.

"I think he's exactly the right man for her," his mother replied pertly. "He's handsome, titled and generous. Not to mention, good natured," she added with a smirk in Nate's direction, no doubt to make sure the barb struck.

It had and Nate stiffened. Yes, he could be a tad overbearing at times but his responsibilities had made him so. And he knew how to be good natured, he really did!

"But he began this as a bet," he said.

"He did confess everything to me. And he'd intended to marry me from the start," Fiona said thoughtfully, biting her lip.

"He's honest too," his mother announced, spreading her arms with a theatrical flourish.

Nate saw red.

"He's just not right for you, Fiona," he repeated, not bothering to address her formally. He'd touched her and kissed her for god's sakes and he was tired of pretending otherwise.

"I might never get the chance to marry again, your grace. It's nothing short of a miracle that the Earl wants to marry someone like me."

"What do you mean someone like you?"

"Mousy, without any bloodlines to recommend me..."

"You're perfectly beautiful and any man would be lucky to have you," he growled.

Fiona's mouth opened and closed like a fish and his mother was watching him intently.

Good God, what the hell was wrong with him?!

"You think I'm beautiful?" she squeaked.

"Of course," he said gruffly, annoyed that she had to ask. And she was. Her beauty wasn't overtly apparent as Sophia's.

Her beauty was more understated. It lay in the simplicity of her features. He'd thought her plain in the beginning, but then he'd started to notice her more closely.

Her eyes were so dark, he often found himself getting lost in their depths—he knew without a shadow of doubt that he could spend hours just looking into her eyes. Her nose was tiny, giving her a pixie like appearance. But her mouth was plump and pink—and it tasted as good as strawberries. He knew, he'd tasted them.

She was such a petit little thing but she fit well with him. Her hair was perfect—dark like her eyes and soft as silk.

She suited him perfectly. And it had felt like she'd been made for him when he'd been kissing her yesterday.

But Nate had discovered that feelings had no place in this real world.

No matter how much he fantasised about her in his dreams at night and no matter how much he enjoyed her company during the day, what he wanted could never be.

He supposed he could make her his mistress—he wanted her that badly. But he wouldn't be able to live with himself if he did such a thing to his wife. And he knew that Fiona would feel the same way.

"If I were a man, Fiona, I would snatch you right up before anyone else could," his mother said, eyeing him meaningfully.

Was his mother trying to tell him something? It didn't make any sense.

"You're biased," Fiona laughed, joining his mother by the bed.

They made such a pretty picture, his mother and Fiona so comfortable and happy to spend time with each other. His heart clenched with longing... longing to join them.

He could never imagine Sophia wanting to spend time with his mother willingly. Hell she hardly spoke two words whenever they met. He'd always thought that his mother was a difficult woman, that she wouldn't allow anyone close to her. But he'd been wrong.

He'd heeded to Fiona's advise and had begun to pay more attention to his mother. He'd been surprised to see the change in her—and himself. He enjoyed talking with her. His mother, it seemed had a deadly sense of humour. It was as if he was rediscovering her.

He felt like an arse for ignoring her all this while.

Fiona had given him the greatest gift, he realised. And he loved her for it.

He loved her.

The realisation came to him like a splash of cold water. He had to leave.

He turned to tell the ladies that he was leaving but they appeared to be lost in whatever conversation they were having so he slipped out quietly.

He'd really bungled it this time.

Lusting after his mother's companion had been bad enough.

But now he was in love with the most troublesome woman in England.

Nate didn't know if he wanted to laugh or cry. Never had he imagined that he would find love. He'd always assumed that he'd find a woman he could be comfortable with—one who'd make a good duchess. Just his luck that the one woman he did fall in love with couldn't be his duchess.

He wanted to rail at the unfairness of it all.

But his fate had been sealed when he'd been born to this dukedom.

Chapter 19

S ophia twirled before her mirror.

Oh but she looked fine, she thought with a satisfied smirk. Surely no one in this silly house party could hold a candle to her even on her worst days. But today...

She grinned.

Nathaniel would take one look at her and forget about that little witch Butterworth.

But the thought of the companion reduced some of her good humour. She was a nuisance. Had she not been here, Sophia would've had that ring on her finger.

She'd decided to keep her pink taffeta for when Nathaniel would announce their nuptials. But it seemed like he'd forgotten the purpose of this house party, she thought bitterly. And so she'd worn her best gown with the most expensive pearls tonight.

The ton would see her for who she was. That Butterworth could try and act as sweet and friendly as she liked, but the moment Sophia turned on her charm, the ton would forget about the inconsequential companion. Of that she was confident.

Soon she'd be the Duchess of Bedford. She would own this mansion and its surrounding lands. She'd have several estates and more money than she could ever spend. She'd be the most sought after woman in London.

Of course, there was the small problem of Nathaniel's mother—he did seem unnecessarily attached to her. But she could remedy that.

Sophia was generous, surely she could spare the dower house to the old crone. She could rusticate there while Sophia attended balls on Nathaniel's arm.

She sighed happily.

Life was just going to get better.

Once she disposed of the companion.

***************"You look well, tonight," Nate said to Fiona when she appeared for that evening's entertainments. She was wearing some cream coloured confection with a low bodice and he couldn't help but stare at her. Now that he'd realised that he loved her, it had become harder to resist her allure. He wanted to hide her, to keep her all to himself. He didn't want those other gentlemen to chase her.

"So do you," she smiled faintly and Nate found that his face had heated under the influence of her compliment.

Her eyes sparkled with mischief and sadness—he knew that didn't make sense but that was Fiona. For such a talkative woman, she could also convey all of her emotions with her wide eyes. And he knew her, understood her. He also suspected the reasons for her sorrow. It could either be him or Winston that had caused trouble to her mind.

He wanted to erase that world weary look from her face. He wanted her to smile widely, the way she had when he'd reluctantly agreed to hire her for two weeks. Or when he'd told her that her beloved romance novels had arrived. He was also particularly fond of the expression she'd worn just after he'd kissed her—dazed and surprised.

But he had no right to see those wonderful things, they both knew that.

The Dukedom came first, he reminded himself sternly.

And yet he found himself enquiring after things he had no business enquiring after. "What have you thought about Winston's proposal?"

"I have asked him for some time...as your mother suggested."

Nate wanted to roar his frustration.

"Winston's not an option, Fiona."

"Would you rather I marry someone like Lord Burns who is thrice my age or Sir Percy who is sure to gamble away what is left of his inheritance?" she asked hotly.

"You don't marry at all," he snapped.

Her face closed up immediately and Nate was shocked by the extent of his selfishness.

"I see how much concern you have about my future and it heartens me, your grace. However, I shall have to consider Lord Winston not only because he the best option I have but also because I hold him in high regard," she said before storming off.

She held him in low regard, Nate knew even though she hadn't said it out loud.

Now he'd gone and made things worse. She would probably say yes to Winston just to spite him. He wanted to go after her and say...something. But he knew there was nothing he could do to take back his thoughtless words.

He turned around only to find his nemesis standing before him.

"Good evening, your grace. Have you happened to see Fiona anywhere?" Winston came up to Nate.

"No," he replied stiffly. Nate was tempted to reach out and grab the young man by his neck for even saying her name.

"Tell her I'm looking for her if you see her, will you? She said she'll give me her answer tonight. I'm almost positive she'd say yes," Winston grinned boyishly and rushed off. Nate had tried hard to find something on his face—something that suggested that this was all a game to the man. But all he'd found was sincere hope.

If anything, this only made him feel worse.

What right did he have to stop Fiona from marrying Winston when he was prepared to offer her what Nate couldn't?

A sudden thought struck Nate. What if he did throw caution to the winds and marry the woman he wanted? The woman that he loved...

He dismissed the thought immediately.

He was already betrothed to Sophia for heaven's sake. He couldn't just call it off.

"Nathaniel, I've been looking for you," Sophia called out.

Nate closed his eyes and took a deep breath before opening them.

Of course, she looked lovely. But he felt nothing, not even a slight admiration. He knew of the effect she had on the other men, but it did absolutely nothing for him.

"Good evening, Sophia."

"Aren't you going to tell me how I look?" she fluttered her fan before her face coyly.

"You look beautiful," he said dutifully. She giggled and Nate thought that if he had to listen to that sound got the rest of his life, he'd probably tear his ears out.

He'd rather listen to Fiona sing.

"I saw Miss Butterworth going off somewhere with Lord Winston. I suppose she's going to accept his proposal," she said, smiling like Fiona and her were old friends.

Nate clenched his teeth.

"Where did they go?"

"I don't know. I couldn't follow them, obviously. I might have interrupted on their private moments," she said conspiratorially and slid closer to his side.

Now he was positive he looked close to exploding.

He was about to go in search of Fiona and that cretin Winston when they heard a commotion coming from above stairs.

Nate raced up the stairs.

On the floor lay his mother, her face twisted in pain and gasping for breath. Some guests surrounded her but looked unsure of how to help her.

Nate picked her up, flinching when she groaned and carried her to her chamber. He asked Winterbottom to call for a physician and stayed by his mother's side.

"How did this happen?" he asked his mother when Fiona entered the chamber, her face creased with worry. But Nate wasn't fooled.

Chapter 20

"Yes, what happened, your grace?" Fiona rushed to his mother's side.

"Look at her pretending like this wasn't all her fault. She shouldn't have left your mother alone for her romantic tête-à-tête in the first place," Sophia whispered from beside him. He felt his palms fist up of their own accord.

"I had just exited my room when I felt someone bump into me. It was unexpected and I lost my balance," his mother replied to them both.

"I'll go find something for the pain," Fiona said briskly and left the chamber.

"I shall return in a moment, mother," Nate kissed her forehead and followed Fiona, shutting the door on his way out.

"Miss Butterworth," he called. She turned around immediately. "You are dismissed," he said shortly, wishing they weren't surrounded by his curious guests.

"What do you mean?" she looked confused.

"I mean that my mother no longer requires your services."

"Nate..." she came forward, her hand stretched out.

"You shall address him as your grace. Only his equals are allowed to call him by his name name," Sophia said, appearing at his side. Nate said nothing.

Fiona looked like he'd slapped her but Nate didn't budge.

He'd trusted her with his mother's safety and this is how she'd repaid him. She'd abandoned his mother in hopes of finding a brighter future as Winston's countess.

Then she'd already made her choice, so this was all just a formality anyway.

"May I at least know on what grounds you've decided to dismiss me?" she whispered shakily, her hands clenched by her sides.

"Not that I owe you any explanation but you chose a romantic interlude with your lover over your duty to my mother. She fell because you weren't there to take care of her."

"What are you talking—"

"Oh don't make a fool of yourself anymore than you already have, Miss Butterworth. I had really started to like you. But I suppose your lack of breeding was bound to show someday," Sophia said snidely.

Fiona was shooting daggers at Sophia and Nate just wanted her gone from his sight.

He couldn't believe he'd actually given such a selfish woman his heart.

"At least allow me to care for her grace until she recovers. And then I will leave," she said stonily.

"I'll have the best of England's physicians if need be," Nate said and turned around.

"And if it's your wages you're worried about, they will be delivered to you by tomorrow morn," Sophia said to Fiona. Nate turned around immediately. There was no need to insult her this way, after all...

But she was gone, running down the stairs even as she swiped at her face with the back of her arm.

Every instinct in his body told him to chase her. But he had other things on his mind—like seeing to his mother's comfort.

****

Nate couldn't sleep that night. All he could think of was Fiona's face when Sophia had said those things to her and he hadn't stopped her. He was beginning to feel like a real ass.

But then he'd have this image of Fiona in a passionate embrace with her beau while his mother lay on the floor—helpless and in pain.

So he alternated between anger and guilt.

God he really wished he didn't love her. It just hurt so much thinking about the last month. He'd never thought that he could feel so strongly about a person...

Meanwhile, Fiona was crying herself sick.

Oh but she hated him. He had to be the most despicable, cold hearted, unreasonable, wicked man alive with an equally wicked fiancé to go with.

They were perfect for each other. The untouchable Lady Sophia and her untouchable stupid Duke, she punctuated the thought with another punch to her pillow.

She hated him. She hated the fact that the first and probably the last man she'd even loved this way had to be such an ass.

She'd been in love for God's sake! Yes, it was doomed from the start and she was often sad but still—why did he have to go and ruin it like this?

Or maybe this wasn't such a bad thing. He'd certainly made hating him a lot more easier.

But the point was moot. She wasn't going to see him and the duchess ever again. He'd made sure of that.

Her heart twisted painfully in her chest.

Well, she wasn't going to get out of this unscathed.

****

"Why haven't I seen Fiona after last night?!" his mother was bellowing at a maid when he entered her chamber the next morning.

"Mother," he interrupted and signalled the maid to leave—who looked beyond relieved as she swept a quick curtsy and dashed out.

"I trust you're feeling better?" he asked pulling a chair next to her.

"I won't feel better until I know where Fiona is, son."

"You won't see her again, mother. I dismissed her," he sighed heavily, the pain from his wound was still fresh.

"You dismissed her? Are you daft?" his mother exploded.

"It's not so bad—"

"Nathaniel, she was the best thing that ever happened to me after your father's death."

"I'm sure there are dozens of other companions who are way better at their jobs than Miss Butterworth was," he said placatingly.

"She's not just a companion to me, Nathaniel," his mother said quietly. "May I at least know why you did this?"

"Isn't is obvious? She wasn't doing her job. Look what happened last night because of her mistake."

"What are you saying? She was only fetching my cane because I'd forgotten it somewhere. She'd specifically asked me to stay where I was while she got it because I haven't been very steady on my feet. And I did stay there. It's just that someone came onto to me suddenly—which was strange and I fell."

"She wasn't fetching you anything. She was meeting Winston—to tell him yes," Nate said dumbly.

"I can't believe you dismissed her in a fit if jealousy," his mother groaned.

"Jealousy? What are you talking about?"

"I know you love her so you can quit pretending otherwise," she snapped. "And all this poppycock about Winston is exactly that—poppycock. Why don't you ask him yourself? As you should've before attacking that poor girl."

Nate didn't even have time to be shocked that his mother knew everything because he was already out of his chair—headed to find Winston.

Chapter 21

"Of course she didn't agree to marry me!" Winston exploded exasperatedly.

"And you never saw her that evening?" Nate asked again.

"No, I did not."

"Good," Nate sighed, relieved.

"What did you say?" Winston narrowed his eyes.

"I said that I'm sorry," Nate cleared his throat. "Is there anything else about last night that you found peculiar?"

"I've told you everything, Duke," Winston groaned. "I was looking for Fiona and right after I asked you, Lady Sophia told me that she saw Fiona heading towards the balcony. I went there but there was nobody there. I suppose Lady Sophia must've been mistaken. Now if you'll excuse me, I need to go find some whiskey."

Nate was too stunned to speak and let him go.

Sophia had told Winston that? Hadn't she told him that she'd seen them speaking to each other in private.

Warning bells went off in his head and he began to feel the truth dawning on him.

Fiona was innocent. He'd even seen the walking stick in her hand when she'd entered his mother's chamber that night. She'd been trying to tell him and his mother had told him but he'd let his own jealousy and Sophia's comments blind him to the truth.

But he couldn't confront Sophia only on the basis of his suspicions.

Very well, he'd just talk to her.

"Your grace, beg pardon but I would request you to come to the library," Winterbottom said, approaching him.

"What is it?" Nate asked him, not liking the expression on his butler's usually expressionless face.

"After her grace fell last night, I couldn't sleep all night, your grace. And the fact that you held Miss Butterworth responsible didn't sit with me either..."

"And?" Nate raised one eyebrow.

"So I asked questions all morning and have discovered the real culprit."

He pushed open the door to the library and found a footman standing inside.

"Him?" Nate asked dubiously.

"He was the one who knocked her down, your grace," Winterbottom nodded.

"Why?" Nate asked even as he quickly marched towards the younger man and caught hold of his collar.

"Somebody made me do it, your grace! I had no personal vengeance," the boy stuttered.

"Who?" Nate spat.

The footman swallowed uncomfortably and licked his dry lips but said nothing.

"Tell me and I'll not kill you for hurting my mother," Nate said menacingly.

"It was Becca, she said her mistress would make her life miserable if she didn't have this job done," the footman finally said and sagged. "And I love Becca!" he puffed up his chest.

Nate let him go and the boy crumpled to the floor. "Who the devil is Becca?!"

"She's a Lady's maid."

"Which Lady?" Nate growled impatiently.

"Lady Sophia's."

Winterbottom looked horrified but Nate wasn't very surprised. He'd already suspected that Sophia was behind all this. The question was why.

He asked Winterbottom to dismiss the boy and exited the library. He had to find that fiancé of his. She owed him some answers.

As he'd suspected, he found her in the main hall, surrounded by her bevy of admirers.

"Sophia, we need to talk."

"Oh Nathaniel! There you are. How is your mother? I couldn't sleep all night after seeing her in so much pain," she pouted and put a hand to her heart with a dramatic flourish.

"As it happens, I intend to speak of her," Nate replied curtly.

"Of course," she tittered nervously and slid her hand up his arm. He lead her out and towards the gardens.

"What is it? You're making me nervous," she smiled when they finally reached the gardens.

"Why did you have that footman push my mother down? Was it because of your jealousy towards Fiona?"

Her eyes widened in fear. "What are you saying, Nathaniel?! I would never do that to your mother!"

"Either you tell me here or I question you in front of all the guests. Before all of your peers."

She seemed to think for a few moments, her hands fluttering by her sides.

"Fine. I did it."

"Why?" Nate growled.

"Because I hate her! I kept asking you to stay away from that worthless companion but you didn't listen."

"Get out of my sight. And don't ever try to speak to me again."

"But Nate, I did this for us!" She wailed and latched onto his arm. "How could we have had a happy marriage if that companion lived in this house?! Not that I intended to stay here at all but we would visit your mother for Christmas and—"

"What?" he asked, cutting her off. She swallowed at the dangerously low volume of his voice.

"It's just that at her age, London would exhaust her. Surely you see that..." she hedged.

"Yes, London would exhaust her. Which was why I intended to stay here 'round the year. With my mother," Nate said firmly and drew away her grasping hands from his arm. "You are the worst woman I've ever had the displeasure of meeting, Lady Sophia. I rue the day I proposed to you but at least I saw your true colours now."

"I suppose I have Fiona to thank for that, along with many other things," Nate added more softly.

"She's the reason all this is happening!" Sophia wailed pitifully.

"Is she? If you would've told me that you wished to dismiss her, as my duchess you would've had every right to ask that of me. Instead you chose to go about this in a backhanded manner. You even attempted to hurt my mother."

"Nathaniel, surely you can forgive me!"

"I cannot. So you either go back to the hall, tell everyone that you've chosen to call off our wedding, pack your things and leave or I can tell everyone about what you've done and ruin your reputation in the ton."

"You wouldn't!" her eyes widened with disbelief.

"I assure you, I most definitely would."

"And then what? Marry your stupid companion?" Sophia spat.

"If she'll still have me, yes," he said softly. "And you speak of my future duchess, Lady Sophia. So I suggest you exercise some restraint on how you address her."

"She's not as good as me."

"Yes, she's even better. Hell, I wouldn't degrade her by comparing her to you. Now you may leave," Nate inclined his head.

Sophia turned around and stormed off.

Nate felt a huge weight being lifted off his chest. Now all he had to do was apologise to Fiona and ask her if she loved him as much as he loved her.

As simple as that sounded, Nate knew that it was a task of mammoth proportions.

Chapter 22

"You cannot see her, your grace," the woman declared, one of her hands resting on her hip and the other on a worn walking stick.

Nate was currently standing outside of Fiona's home. He'd come to grovel. This woman had answered the door and had immediately denied him the permission to enter when she'd learnt his identity.

Guessing from the authoritative look on her face and her white hair, she had to be Fiona's infamous great grandmother.

He knew he should be appalled but he was merely amused.

"But I need to speak with her," he tried again.

"I don't think she wants you to speak to her," she huffed. "Don't you think you've said enough?"

Nate stiffened.

Being reminded of his stupidity hurt.

"Yes, I said some things that I regret. And I have come to apologise. And tell her I love her."

"You what?" the older woman's mouth practically fell open.

"I do. I love her with every breath in my body," he said solemnly. "I was blinded by jealousy when I said those things to her."

Her face softened just a little and Nate took advantage and ploughed on.

"I wish to marry her and make her my duchess for I cannot imagine anyone else filling that position anymore. It has to be her..."

"You don't play fair, Duke," she huffed, disgruntled.

Nate grinned.

"I still don't think she'll want to see you," Jeanette warned as she opened the door wider to let him in.

"Where is she?" he asked when he didn't see her anywhere.

"She's gone out to the market. She'll be back any moment now," she smiled slyly.

Bloody hell. Fiona had been out the entire while that he'd spent begging for entrance.

"You don't play fair either," Nate acknowledged the woman.

"Sit down and make yourself comfortable. I'm sure she'll be back any moment now," she repeated. Nate found that odd.

But after waiting for an hour and a half, he understood why.

There was still no sign of Fiona and Nate was beginning to lose patience.

"I'll go find her myself!" he stood up and made his way to the door. Jeanette tried to stop him but he didn't listen. He'd had enough biscuits, tea and inane conversation.

He forcefully opened the door and there stood Fiona, her hand frozen in place as she'd made to open the door.

Nate would've kissed her just then.

Except, she didn't look half as happy to see him as he was to see her.

She looked furious.

"Nana Jeanette! Why is this man in our house?" she shouted.

"I think you should ask him, darling," she replied calmly.

"Why are you here?" she turned to him, her eyes wild.

"I had to apologise—"

"Apology denied. Now leave," she pointed outside.

"You can't speak to me this way."

"Oh that's funny! Because I am speaking to you that way now. So I clearly can."

Nate thought he heard a muffled snort and he turned to stare at Fiona's great grandmother. But the woman covered it with a cough.

"I know you're angry and you have every reason to be. But hear me out... please," he looked to Fiona again.

"I am exhausted and I don't need you to invade my living space and demand to be acknowledged," she replied.

Now that really did it.

"I invaded your living space? Don't you think it's the other way around?! You entered my home and refused to leave. Then you came by every single day and tormented me until I had no choice but to fall in love with you! If anyone forced someone to acknowledge them, it was you. I tried so hard to stay away from you but you weren't having it. You were everywhere. Hell you didn't even spare my bed chamber. You had my entire house smelling like roses. I didn't even know I liked roses so much until you. You, Miss Butterworth even have my mother under your spell, not to mention the entire staff of Bedford manor. And I am no exception," he finished his tirade and found Fiona staring at him while her mouth touched the floor.

He turned around to find Jeanette gone. She'd probably decided to give them both some privacy.

"You love me?" she whispered.

"Yes. And I want to marry you."

There was a long pause after that.

"Well?" He prodded when Fiona refused to speak.

"That didn't quite sound like an apology," she murmured.

"I'm so sorry for last night, Fiona. I was mad with jealousy...when I thought you'd accepted Winston's proposal, that you were with him, I lost it," he sighed.

"That was not the problem. The problem was that you didn't trust me enough to know that I'd never put anything before my duty to your mother. You don't know me at all, Duke. And you need to know someone to love them," Fiona sighed.

"No, don't say that! I made a mistake, Fiona. Please forgive me. I promise I will never repeat it."

"Alright. I forgive you."

"Really?" He went to her and took her hands in his.

"That doesn't mean I love you," she whispered, a frown marring her beautiful face.

She might as well have slapped him.

"You don't?" He asked even as he felt her hands slipping from his.

She wasn't meeting his eyes but she shook her head.

Nate didn't know what to say. He didn't blame her, he really didn't. But this rejection hurt like hell.

He nodded and turned to leave. She didn't stop him.

And so he left, shutting the door softly behind him.

As soon as the Duke left, Fiona ran to her room. She sat on her bed and it creaked familiarly.

I want to marry you, he'd said.

He couldn't possibly mean it, could he?

She was a lowly companion with nothing to recommend her.

And what about Lady Sophia? Had he broken off his betrothal with the Lady for her?

Good god, what was happening in her life?

Two months ago her life had been so simple. Free of such entanglements. She wanted to think but her head had began to throb. So she lay down.

The expression on his face when she'd told him that she didn't love him—ha what a lie that had been—had broken her heart...or whatever was left of it. She didn't want to lie to him but he'd never let her be if he knew that she loved him.

And she knew one thing for certain, she'd never forget the way he'd treated her.

Chapter 23

"Your grace! Your mother was asking for you," Winterbottom stopped Nate when he was going to his room.

"Is everything alright?"

"Yes."

Nate nodded at his butler and headed to his mother's chambers.

"Good evening, mother. You asked for me?" he knocked and entered.

"Yes," she replied and patted the bed, signalling him to come sit. "You left in a hurry this morning."

"About that...mother I have broken off my betrothal with Sophia," he said on a sigh.

"That is wonderful, son!" she surprised him by saying.

"You're not upset? It will cause some talk, after all even though she'll be the one to publicly call it off..."

"Upset? I'm ecstatic, Nathaniel. I knew from day one that she was entirely wrong for you. As for the 'talk', I don't give a squat," she chortled.

Nate was amazed. He'd certainly not expected this reaction.

"This might be the smartest thing you've done in years," she was saying.

Nate was silent.

"I take it you've spoken to Fiona," she prompted.

"I apologised," he said with a nod.

"And?"

"She forgave me."

"Oh." She actually sounded surprised.

"I proposed to her...told her I loved her."

"You're marrying her?" she grinned.

"No, she said she doesn't love me," he replied, dazed. Was his mother actually happy that he wanted to marry her companion?

"Of course she loves you. She's lying," she said confidently.

Nate shook his head a little.

"You're not angry?"

"Angry that you've finally decided to listen to your heart? That you're finally reaching for the happiness that I've always wanted for you?" she admonished.

"I love you, mother," he said.

"I love you too, son," she kissed his cheek. "Now about that rubbish Fiona said...she does love you. Nathaniel."

"If she does, then why would she reject my proposal?"

"Because she still hasn't forgiven you," she smiled slightly. "And rightly so. You behaved like an utter dolt."

When Nate didn't look like he believed her, she sighed.

"I don't want to annoy her. If she'd loved me, I wouldn't have thought twice before grovelling before her until she agreed to be mine. But she doesn't, mother."

Linda wanted to tell her son that he couldn't have been more wrong. She knew Nathaniel and she knew Fiona. One week after her arrival, she'd noticed that something was going on between her son and her companion. She hadn't done anything and had let fate lead the way.

But something told her that it was time she interfered.

"You go on and rest, Nathaniel. I'm sure you've had a long day."

"I have some estate business to take care of," he shook his head. "I can't wait for this house party to get over," he sighed.

"It will be tomorrow night," his mother replied.

Nate smiled and left.

He'd lied about the estate business. He merely intended to get drunk.

He felt like his heart had been ripped open from his chest and he needed some respite. Desperately.

******************The next evening, Bedford manor.

Fiona took a steadying breath and took a step forward.

"Miss Butterworth," Winterbottom announced and several heads turned to look in her direction.

She felt alone, the way she had when she'd first entered this house a few months back.

But she was doing this for the duchess, she reminded herself and pasted a wide smile on her face. And honestly, it was better than she'd anticipated. Of course a majority of people were whispering behind their fans while some were staring quite blatantly. But there were some familiar smiles as well—even Lord Winston offered her a genuine smile. Fiona smiled back.

For what it was worth, she'd at least earned one friend.

He quickly waded through the throng of guests to reach her.

"You look dazzling, Miss Butterworth," he bowed before her and kissed her hand. Well she better did. She was sure this dress cost a fortune—the duchess's fortune. At first she'd felt uncomfortable taking it…it was Nate's money after all but then her grace had practically browbeaten her. And although she'd thought of wearing her own clothes just to defy the duchess, in the end she'd given it. Besides, the dress was too beautiful to set aside.

"So do you, my lord," Fiona chuckled.

"I'm very sorry about what happened the other day—I learned that I was somehow responsible for it," he grumbled.

The reminder of that night immediately sobered her. "Think nothing of it. I'm not."

He didn't look like he believed her but he let it be.

A few more guests talked to her and even asked her if she was still Lady Linda's companion. She didn't know either. Nate had apologised and it didn't seem like the Duchess was done with her either because she'd spent at least two hours in her home trying to convince Fiona to come.

So she'd given them all diplomatic answers.

She didn't want to think about her future anymore. She just wanted to enjoy this one night without any burdens...she wanted to feel the way any normal Lady would at a ball.

Fiona was trying to find the duchess when someone suddenly pulled her to the side. It was dark and she struggled a bit.

She was about to scream but a hand closed over her mouth.

And then she knew who it was. She knew that smell. And she recognised the feel of his body against her back.

Her shoulders immediately sagged in relief and she turned around slowly to face him.

"Good evening, your grace. How can I help you?" she tipped up her head. Just the familiar angles of his face made her chest ache with longing.

"What are you doing here?" Nate asked harshly.

"You can't kick me out this time. I'm her grace's guest," Fiona shot out defensively.

"You misunderstand. Are you here because you've forgiven me? Because you love me?" He asked and the hope in his voice stung.

"No," she whispered. As much as she wanted to tell him that she loved him too, she knew that she didn't belong in his world. She'd always be that impoverished vicar's daughter and he, a grand duke. She was doing him a favour, really. Her and his duchess? It was laughable.

"Then? Are you here to torture me?"

"No. I'm not here for you. I came because your mother asked me to."

"She knows. I think she's known all along."

"Known what?"

"That I love you. She says you love me too but I guess she's wrong about that," he murmured.

"Stop it," she gasped.

"I can't," he said hoarsely as his hand came up to cup her cheek. Fiona resisted the urge to rest her face on that palm, the urge to hold onto him and never let go.

"I can't stop loving you, Fiona."

Then don't, she wanted to say.

"I should go. This is highly improper," she said in a rush.

"You've always been an improper companion," he said and she supposed that amused him for she detected a smile in his voice.

"But I'm not your companion anymore, you made sure of that," she said and pushed him away from her. And then she fled from that darkened hallway.

Chapter 24

"I'm glad you made it," Linda smiled at Fiona.

"I am too," she replied with a slight squeeze to her hand.

"So have you met Nate, then?"

"Yes," Fiona whispered. "He looked terrible."

"Love does that to people," Linda winked conspiratorially.

"Oh stop that, will you? I don't need a reminder of his feelings for me."

"Why-ever not?"

"Because I'll make him a pathetic duchess," she replied pertly.

"That is for me to decide, Miss Butterworth."

Fiona turned abruptly to find Nate standing right behind her. He looked angry for some reason. Very angry. The duchess should've at least warned her that he was standing right behind her, the traitor.

"Eavesdropping isn't something I would've associated with you, your grace," she curtsied, hoping she'd hidden her emotions well.

"And subterfuge wasn't something I'd associated you with," he snapped.

"What do you mean?"

"You do love me, don't you?" He asked bleakly.

"Stop it, you're creating a scene," Fiona said urgently. People were beginning to gather around them. It's not like they were arguing in a private place so she could hardly blame them. But this would cause talk for months...

"I don't care. I don't care about anything but you...it seems I haven't in a while."

"Why are you doing this?"

"Because I want you in my life, Fiona. I love you and the very thought of existing without you by my side makes me sick."

"I'm sorry but—"

"Don't you dare say you don't love me because we all know that's a lie!"

Fiona made to leave, things were getting out of hand. But he stopped her by catching her wrist.

"Let me go," she begged.

"I'm not letting you go again." He gently cupped her cheek and Fiona knew that her facade of being unaffected was falling apart.

"I was an imbecile to let you go the first time. And I'd be damned if I did it again," he said seriously. He was staring into her eyes, looking at her as if she was the only person in the room...as if she was all that mattered.

After that, Fiona didn't care who was watching them. Because all that mattered to her was this man too.

"Do you love me?" He asked again.

"Of course, I do, you silly goose," she groaned, defeated. But the smile he gave her was so breathtaking that she didn't mind losing just this once.

"That doesn't change the fact that I'd not be the kind of duchess you'd envisioned for yourself, Nate."

"That is utter rubbish and—" he began but she held up her hand.

"Let me say this. I'm not poised and genteel like Lady Sophia. Nor am I as beautiful. I don't have the connections or wealth to recommend me. I don't sing like an angel or dance gracefully. And I'm so very clumsy—God knows I owe you at least seven new vases and sculptures. I don't even speak French well." Fiona was out of breath by the time she finished. Her Duke merely looked amused by her diatribe.

"Well its a good thing that I understand English perfectly well, then," he grinned.

"Nate—" she began frustratedly but this time he didn't let her finish. His face immediately became more serious.

"Fiona, if I wanted poise and grace, I would've married Sophia. Granted, I had thought that I wanted those things in my life. But then I realised that all those things would bore me to death. They wouldn't bring me the same happiness that you do."

"I agree, you don't sing like an angel...that is a gross understatement," he chuckled. "But angelic or no, that is the only sound I wish to hear. You're wrong about one thing...you have any number of things to recommend you."

"Like?"

"You're so kind and giving, Fiona. You're extremely smart and caring. Not to mention, lovable. I think every member of the Bedford household is in love with you."

Fiona grinned at that even though tears were streaming down her face. Nate gently wiped them away with his thumbs.

"There's no one I'd rather make my duchess, Fiona."

"Really?" she croaked out.

He nodded.

"But you deserve someone better. You deserve the best, Nate."

"You are the best. At least for me."

"That is a very romantic thing to say, isn't it?" Fiona turned around and asked the duchess even as she wiped at the tears on her cheeks.

"It is!" Linda nodded approvingly.

"So tell me, Miss Butterworth. Will you do me the very great honour of becoming my wife?" he asked and knelt down before her.

There were collective gasps from the crowd but Fiona was too happy to care.

And then she remembered.

"You shall have to ask for Nana's permission," she replied sheepishly.

He was stunned for a moment but then he broke into a dazzling smile.

"So you'll marry me if Jeanette agrees?"

"Yes," she laughed. Actually, she would marry him even if the whole world stood against them. But she had a feeling Nana Jeanette would agree. She did seem to have a weak spot when it came to handsome dukes, after all.

"To Nana Jeanette's then," he announced, already dragging her out. "And on our way there, you can tell me how much you love me and how very happy you are."

"Alright," she grinned.

As they raced out, there were several cheers and claps from the guests. Linda sat back in her chair, extremely satisfied with the turn of events.

"Congratulations, you grace," Winterbottom murmured to her from beside her. He looked satisfied as well. "You don't look very surprised."

"You don't either," she raised one brow.

"To be honest, your grace," Winterbottom flushed guiltily, "I have been hoping for this outcome for a while now."

"I have too, Winterbottom. I have too," she winked.